The Wolf and the Butterfly

Black Hills Wolves Book 19

By
Kerry Adrienne

This book is a work of fiction. Names, characters, places, and incidents are the products of the author's imagination or used fictitiously. Any resemblance to actual events, locales or persons, living or dead, is entirely coincidental.

ISBN: 978-1-68361-041-0
Cover art by Fiona Jayde

Published by Decadent Publishing Company, LLC
Look for us online at:
www.decadentpublishing.com

Dedication

To Rebecca Royce—I'm honored to call you friend. Thank you for everything.

Chapter One

B*lood.*

Nika rested his front paws on the warm, rough rock and scented the air. His hackles rose, bristling at the trespasser.

Wolf.

He tilted his head and took another whiff to be sure. The fragrance of late summer's buttercups and honeysuckle floated atop the breeze, overpowered by the coppery tang of blood and the musky odor of Wolf.

Female.

His ears pricked to attention. First day as pack scout and he'd found something out of order near Los Lobos. Something *wrong*. His heart hammered when he breathed in the information carried on the air.

Danger.

The smells pulled at him, and he paced. Being a scout required him to trot the perimeter woods of Los Lobos and report anything out of place. He'd trained hard and had been so excited to be promoted. Scout was a lot of responsibility, and he couldn't screw it up.

Not on his first day. He sniffed, trying to sort out the signals on the wind.

Pain.

Nika whimpered, the faint strains of the she-Wolf's pain branched through his mind like a mosaic of frost on a cold windowpane. She suffered.

He'd been chosen scout in part because he was young and agile, but Gee had singled him out above the others because of his empathic tendencies. He sensed feelings and right then, with his nose to the west, he knew he had to save the hurt she-Wolf.

He sent up a short yip, followed by a high-pitched howl then, as procedure required, repeated the signal. Any pack member within earshot would be alerted to the potential trouble and notify the proper authorities. He'd scouted a thousand yards into the woods before picking up on the scent, so other pack members were close enough to hear his call for help.

Danger. Too close to Los Lobos. He barked the warning one last time, knowing the sound would carry well over the cacophony of insect song.

A brief burst of wind swirled by, carrying dust and crumpled leaves, and the promise of fall. He scanned the forest, listening and hoping to pick up a return call from someone in the pack. He wasn't supposed to go check out the injured Wolf on his own. Protocol dictated he take someone with him to investigate, but if no one was near and he didn't check the situation out, the ramifications could be devastating to the pack.

Besides, the she-Wolf smelled so good, as if she needed him and him alone.

No harm in checking out the situation then reporting his findings.

He bolted toward the injured female, his emotions in all directions from the mixed signals she gave off. His Alpha, Drew, would be proud of him if he handled the threat by himself.

He ran. His paws brushed the ground, and the wind hummed through his lungs, urging him faster.

The setting sun slanted through the dry forest and dust swirled like snow in the streaming sunbeams. Nika smiled a wolf smile, and his heart soared as he slalomed around tree after tree in the dense forest that had been home to wolves since the dawn of time. He panted, and his muscles burned with the delicious warmth of exertion. Being free, running at top speed through the woods, even toward danger, invigorated him.

He slowed to sniff again, adjusted his course, and ran. His tail swung straight behind him when he leapt over fallen limbs and dashed into the head of the valley where the White Spring ran cold and crackled through the rock-lined hills.

Wet.

The smells of fresh water, mud, and fish overwhelmed his nose. He stopped and scanned. Where was she? The scent still played through the air like a counterpoint to late summer's melody of wildflowers. Every cell in his body strained to hear her, smell her, feel her.

His ears pricked at a slight moan from up ahead. *There!* He trotted toward the sound. Gee's voice played in his head on an endless loop. *The pack helps each other. We do things together. Only Ryker works alone.* He pushed the words away.

He dipped his head, his tongue lolling. He panted to cool himself. Fall temperatures would be a welcome change, and even running in the snowiest winter felt better than this summer heat.

He scanned as he moved. Gee wasn't here, nor were Drew or Ryker or anyone else. The duty to protect the pack fell to him, then.

I can handle this female. I am Wolf.

Nika stilled and listened.

Alive.

Her heart beat, thumping a steady rhythm, unfazed by her injury. He zeroed in on where her smell led him, and crept forward. Her faint moans gave away her position, and the coppery tang of blood flooded the air when he neared. She lay on the ground beside a large boulder, her back toward him, and her long, black hair splaying in the mud like broken reeds.

His body screamed *run to her*, but he held back, trotting in a wide circle around her, checking for any other threat. No tracks, human or Wolf, besides hers.

She was alone, Wolf, and injured.

Unshifted and dangerous.

He circled her once more, to double check no one

else was near, and then climbed above her onto the boulder. Her small form was thin, and she had skin not quite as deep brown as his own, though reddish. Native American, no doubt. Probably Lakota Sioux, since their reservation was nearby. But what was she doing in this area of the woods, so close to Los Lobos? This wasn't her territory. Rarely did Lakota wander through these woods without the Alpha's permission. And why wasn't she in Wolf form? Her healing would be much more rapid if she shifted.

He cocked his head and pawed at the boulder, his claws scratching against the rock. He was unsure of what to do. He could send another signal, but she would know he was there.

She moved and struggled to lift up on her elbow. She pushed the hair from her eyes and stared straight at him.

And screamed.

He jumped backward on the boulder, flattening his ears against the piercing sound. So much for not being seen. Rookie mistake. Good thing Gee wasn't near enough to see. He'd put him back in training.

"Go away." She flung a pebble at him. It bounced along the boulder like a rock skipping along the water's surface. Fear radiated from her in thick waves and pummeled his psyche. He wanted to comfort her, take care of her, explain he wasn't a threat. He shook his head. What was he thinking? What made him want to talk to the enemy? She was beautiful, but....

All things unknown are potential dangers to the pack. Especially outsiders.

He backed away, his snout twitching. His dark-brown Wolf form, not large in the Wolf world, but huge to a human, likely scared her, even though she was a Wolf. Injured, she was likely delirious.

Always be wary of unfamiliar Wolves.

Maybe if he shifted, she wouldn't be so afraid. Shifting was yet another reason he'd been a good candidate for Scout—he could transform at will, not something all Wolves could do. He'd had to practice changing and work hard to control the process, but by the time he was sixteen, he'd mastered shifting on demand, and he was pretty proud of his ability.

He trotted out of her sight and concentrated on his human form.

Saliva filled his mouth, and he longed to howl. His Wolf did not want to hide in this dangerous situation.

Not now. You'll scare her even more.

He closed his eyes and savored the slipping of beast into man. Electricity shot through the air in jolts of blue and purple and sounds muffled. Like a long string of hot taffy forming and reforming at the hand of an expert cook, his body plied and flowed into his human shape.

Wolf essence poured into a human-shaped cup.

He opened his eyes and took a deep breath. He breathed almost sterile air when he was human. Colors weren't quite as vibrant around him, but he'd be used to the differences within minutes. He did welcome lesser hearing in human form because the sounds of bugs in the forest sometimes drove him nuts.

He flexed his fingers, stretching out the warmth and numbness accompanying his shift. He checked to see if his clothing had rematerialized. Yep. T-shirt, jeans, and Converse sneakers—confining, but very much normal for a human.

Let's try this again. He put on his best smile and finger-combed his hair.

"Hello?" Nika kept his voice low and calm as he approached the wounded female. If she shifted and attacked, he'd only have a split second to do the same, or risk being torn apart by her Wolf. Any Wolf would win against him in human form, so he was extra cautious, and nothing was more dangerous than an injured Wolf. He moved from behind the rock to the grass beside her.

Curled into a fetal position on a bed of leaves, she didn't look threatening. Her pale yellow dress was pulled taut around her, and she covered her face with her hands. She wore curious leather slippers—one of which lay in the dirt near her legs.

"I won't hurt you." He cocked his head to listen, then shook off the wolfish gesture. "What happened?" He knelt. Even in his human form, he sensed her Wolf, her fear, her utter *femaleness*. Something deep, savage, compelled him to touch her, hold her, *mate* with her. He shuddered, and feral desire rushed through him.

What the hell?

"Go...away," she whispered.

"No. You need my help." He edged closer, his knees near hers. Heat flowed off her, and he leaned forward to savor the warmth piercing straight to his soul. Being so near felt right, like he'd known her forever, and for a moment, he wanted to lie down beside her.

He wagged his head with more force than necessary and backed up a little. He didn't know this she-Wolf, and his duty was to keep pack safety foremost in his thoughts. Impress everyone, especially Drew, with his scouting abilities. The pack Alpha was more of a father figure than anyone in his life. He wanted Drew's respect. Prove he was man enough to take his place in the pack. Earn the title, Scout, and no longer be little orphan Nika who always needed someone to take care of him.

She laid still, her short, shallow breaths punctuated by sobs. Someone so small couldn't be a risk to the pack—right? He looked left to right, but saw no one. Not an ambush.

Might should've double-checked, Nika.

"Why are you alone in the forest? And what's your name?" He winced at his high-pitched tone. He had to stay in control. Gee had warned him his hormones would soon surge and the urge to mate would overtake him. But he hadn't told him he'd act like a blithering idiot around a female he just met.

An injured and possibly dangerous one.

Some scout he was. Alone, babbling, and rocking a hard-on.

"Kimi." The woman pushed the hair from her face and peered at him with beautiful large, brown eyes. Her nose made a regal line down to full lips, holding no hint of a smile. "Please go. You don't want to be around me."

His mouth hung open and he couldn't do a damn thing about it. The woman's gaze held him in a thrall so tight he froze. *Think.* "Of course I do." He licked his lips. "My name's Nika."

Awkward.

She sat up, wincing when she held her arm close to her side. An open sore, red and angry, dripped down her forearm. No wonder he smelled blood. Was it a gunshot wound? Were there hunters nearby?

"Back away from the female, Nika." Drew's voice rang through the woods and snapped him out of his trance.

He scurried backward, bumping into something solid. The werebear, Gee, towered behind him.

I'm fucked.

"Get up." Gee grabbed him under the arms and yanked him to standing. "Looks like you found some trouble."

His heart pounded in his throat.

"What the hell is going on?" Drew paced, his breath coming in short bursts. "I'm all for being a good scout, but I think you forgot some of your training."

He snuck a glance at Kimi. She sat, staring straight ahead, rocking.

"Speak." Gee's voice rattled through him.

The old werebear didn't often show annoyance, though Nika sensed his moods similar to how others might get a taste of cologne in the air. Only annoyance didn't smell good, it smelled like rotting potatoes. Drew was pissed, and Gee wasn't far behind.

He swallowed. "I-I was out scouting. I was supposed to patrol the forest. I hadn't gone far when I scented the injured female. I sounded the alert and came to check things out." Nika dipped his head in submission. Thank the gods Drew was in human form. "I figured I could handle the situation. Since I'm a full scout now. I wanted to show you I could handle things all on my own."

Drew growled and pointed to Kimi. "Why didn't

you send out another alert when you found her? You know that's what you're supposed to do. I have no doubt Gee made procedures clear."

"I figured I could handle an injured female. I didn't think—"

"Exactly." Drew scowled. "You didn't think. Maybe *I* think you aren't ready to scout on your own. We've got to protect Los Lobos, you know that. We can't risk our pack's safety."

"He's young, Alpha." Gee turned to Nika and drew himself up to his six-foot-seven height. "You know better than to engage on your own." Gee sniffed the air and wrinkled his nose. "Sometimes the biggest threats come in the smallest and prettiest packages."

"He didn't do anything wrong," Kimi said.

Gee swung his head to look at her so fast she dropped her gaze. "We're not talking to you right now, clear?"

She nodded.

Gee turned. "I taught you better."

"Yes...." He stared at the ground. The first time he had a little responsibility he blew it. "I'm sorry, Alpha, Gee. I've failed you both."

Drew snorted and kicked at the ground. "Now,

we have to fix this somehow. You've put the pack in a delicate situation."

"She needs medical attention." Gee kneeled beside Kimi, his heavy form folding on itself as he positioned himself on the ground. "She's sick." He examined her arm. "Gravely ill."

She whimpered but didn't pull away.

Nika longed to comfort her. He held back. Gee knew what he was doing, and the last thing he should do was interfere. He was in enough trouble already.

"Drive her away from here. Far away from Los Lobos. The humans will help her if you take her to one of their hospitals." Drew spat on the ground. "We'll figure out what lessons Nika needs to repeat so he can remember to put the pack first."

He peeked at Drew. The Alpha, always strong, wasn't being cruel. He had to protect them all, and he respected him for that. But not much hurt worse than the disappointment on Drew's face.

"She needs more than a human healer can handle." Gee frowned. "Nika and I will take her for treatment."

"Not to Los Lobos. Take her far away." Drew stood over Kimi, his hands on his hips. "She's caused enough disruption around here, dragging us all out into the woods when we have other things we need to be doing. She's a threat to the pack—anyone in our territory is. Besides, we don't even know her story."

She moaned, and Nika's heart sped. He kept quiet, letting the older pack members sort out what was to be done. His body ached with the need to be near her, but he held himself in check. A wrong move, and he could end up in an even worse situation. His place in the pack was one of deference to the Alpha. Always. No matter what he wanted, his Alpha's wishes came first. That's how things worked in the pack.

"I know a healer." Gee stood.

"Who?" Drew asked. "Not too close?"

"Her name is Wen. She works alone, deep in the Black Hills sanctuary. Nowhere near Los Lobos."

Drew nodded. "Perfect. Nika, I want you to think about what might have happened if we hadn't been close by to handle this situation. Not only could our pack's safety have been an issue, but you could've been killed."

"Yes, Alpha."

"Gee will remind you of the procedures, and next

time, you'll follow them."

Nika nodded.

"We'll leave now. I can carry this female." Gee sighed.

"Very good." Drew stuck his hands in his pockets.

"Kill her." The deep voice, though quiet, thundered through the clearing. The birds stopped chattering.

Ryker.

Where the fuck had he come from? The Enforcer leaned against a tree, arms crossed and scowling. Nika shuddered, remaining quiet. The last Wolf in the world he wanted to piss off was Ryker.

"No, we can't kill her." Gee shook his head. "She's our little Nika's mate."

He blinked. Had he heard Gee correctly? *Mate*? He swallowed hard. No, no way the she-Wolf was his mate—she wasn't even a pack member. And he wasn't old enough. Well, he was, but he wasn't ready to settle down. She was gorgeous and made his body act independent of his mind.

Mate? No.

Drew harrumphed. "Well then, that complicates

things."

Kimi tried to sit up, collapsing when she raised her head.

"I-is she okay?" Nika asked.

Gee leaned his ear over her face and paused. "She's breathing." He sat up. "She fainted. We need to go. Wen's got a lot of work ahead of her."

Chapter Two

Kimi kept her eyes closed and feigned unconsciousness. After really fainting when the men stood around in the forest discussing what to do with her, she'd figured pretending was a good ruse while she considered her options. The searing pain in her arm sent shots of white-hot agony from the sore up through her arm every time.

Gee moved forward. His ponytail swayed when he walked, hitting her in the cheek when he stepped over something in his path. She wasn't sure how much longer she could keep pretending. Her father had always told her to listen before speaking, but she was pretty certain this scenario wasn't something he'd ever imagined. She'd left her own world and traveled to another time; it was the only possible explanation. These men had different clothing and spoke another language, though she understood the English of the white man. But where was she? And who were these men?

They thought this awkward, young Wolf was her mate? He wasn't much younger than she, though he acted like he hadn't seen much outside the den. Her blood had run hot when she saw his Wolf. He was good-looking and all the girls would find him attractive. That didn't mean he was her mate for goodness sake.

At least the pain had ebbed from constant agony to occasional bursts. She'd lain on the ground, trying to recuperate enough to move on for who knew how many hours. She'd come to believe the water rushing over the rocks would be the last thing she ever heard. How long had she been traveling before? She didn't even remember. Only the fact she was heading north.

Gee shifted her in his arms, and she scrambled to hold on, not wanting to topple to the ground. So much for pretending she was unconscious. He didn't speak. He pulled her closer. Maybe to offer comfort? He thought more of her than she deserved. She may have infected his Wolf friends, and Nika, even though she'd tried to get him to leave her alone. She tried to warn him, but he wouldn't go away.

Her brain was on repeat. *Mate, mate, mate....*

She'd noticed a pull with Nika, but that couldn't be anything special. She was of age and far from her own tribal pack. What were the odds she'd find her mate now? When she was dying? If this was a trick by the spirits, she didn't find it funny. He couldn't be her mate. In all likelihood, the Bear was trying to set the Wolves with him off guard long enough for him to save her. She sensed how kind he was under his gruff exterior.

"Are we close?" Nika asked.

"Getting there," Gee replied. "Keep walking."

How had she gotten into this predicament? When the sore had appeared on her arm, her father, after consulting the tribe shaman, had sent her north into the new state called South Dakota. Her father wanted someone to travel with her, but the *tunkasila*, Great Spirit, required her to attempt the healing journey alone. She traveled toward the *mni kȟáta*, the "hot water" so sacred to her people, in hopes of curing the disease that had taken so many in her tribe.

"Ooof." She winced as the giant man carrying her stumbled. Tears formed in her eyes, and she blinked them away. Her arm hurt so much. She wasn't scared. His emotions didn't show hostility, like the other men who'd been with him when they found her. And Nika's emotions—he wasn't hostile at all. What she felt from him *did* scare her a little. He was oh so familiar, though she was positive she'd never seen him before.

"Sorry," the Bear-man mumbled. "I'm trying to be careful, but I'm a big man walking a little path."

Nika snickered.

She peeked, and yes, he still followed close to Gee. Despite his odd clothing and coloring, the sight of him prompted a small smile. She shut her eyes again and pictured his wild, curly hair and even wilder golden-brown eyes and soft, brown skin.

In human form, he was handsome. His Wolf had taken her breath away. Her Wolf moaned. Not only was he attractive, but also kind. He hadn't run when she screamed. He'd been thoughtful enough to change form because he thought he frightened her.

Of course Nika's Wolf hadn't scared her. She'd been in and out of consciousness for some time, and when he peered down from the rock over her, she worried he was getting too close. That he might get the illness, too.

"She all right?" Nika asked.

"For now." Gee pulled her tighter in his arms. "But we've got to get help, or she isn't going to survive."

The same words her father had used when he spoke of her illness. Many in her tribe, all Wolf-people, had died. The American forces had pushed them from their homes in the Black Hills. Thought the tribe starved. They were wrong. The United States government provided paltry rations by law and was often a cruel master in individual interactions with the tribe. Too bad the sickness only affected Wolf kind and not land-stealing savages.

"Drew and Ryker weren't happy," Nika said. "I screwed up big time. But she needed me."

"Well, Ryker is rarely happy." Gee laughed. "And you know the Alpha wants to protect the pack. You did screw up, but I understand. You're young, and she's...."

"Let's not talk about that now."

"Agreed. But you'll have to face the truth soon

enough. It's as apparent as the snout on your Wolf's face. She's special to you."

Mate.

No.

She squirmed, and Gee held her tighter.

"Why do you say things like that?" Nika sighed. "What's wrong with her? You said she was sick, not injured."

She listened for the younger man's footsteps. He had to walk fast to keep up with Gee. Too bad he wasn't the one carrying her—she'd love to be in his arms.

Stop thinking about him that way. He's too inexperienced and Father would never approve.

"I have my suspicions." Gee's voice echoed in his chest, and she pressed her head in and listened to his heartbeat, a slow thudding that calmed her pain to almost bearable. "But I want to see what the healer, Wen, says."

"Will she get better?"

"I hope so." Gee paused then continued walking. "But if she has the Wolf sickness, Wen is going to have her work cut out for her."

She squeezed her eyes shut. Gee wasn't going to

like what he found out, if the healer did know anything about this sickness. In her tribe, few survived once they were sick. And Nika could be infected. This Bear-man wasn't at risk, but the Wolf men who'd found her were.

Obviously, they realized she was Wolf even though no mention had been made. She'd known they were Wolf and Bear as soon as they came into the clearing. She wasn't sure they had picked up on her own shifting ability. One of her gifts. She could tell what animal form a person took, by smell, and her ability to sense people had saved her many times in the past.

But not from this sickness. If the shaman was wrong about the hot water, she would die, and maybe many others in her own pack and this pack she'd come across.

And Nika might die, too. If his Wolf had kept on running instead of insisting on helping her, then he'd be safe. She winced. Though she'd only met him, the thought of causing his death seared her heart with a hot brand. If only she wasn't sick, she might be able to help them both. If she could get to the water.

Mate. Her lids heavy, she didn't fight the

thought, letting it drift through her subconscious like a tenuous perfume or partially composed melody.

She must have dozed off because when she woke, the night sky stared at her through scrubby branches. Gee had set her down on soft grass beside a twisted Ponderosa pine, its fragrance sweet like ripe berries. Water rushed over rocks somewhere not far away. Gee and Nika talked somewhere close by, and though she couldn't understand what they said, but their voices soothed her.

The men's footsteps crunched on the dry ground when they approached, and she closed her eyes again.

"Here, you need to drink. You're going to get dehydrated."

She opened her eyes and stared at Nika. He held a small, lit torch in one hand and a cup of some sort in the other.

Mate.

She nodded and opened her mouth to allow him to dribble the liquid between her parched lips. She lapped up the coolness, sad the liquid wasn't the hot water she was looking for, still grateful for the refreshment and his attention. If only she had the strength to sit up.

"*Lila pilamayaye*. Thank you," she whispered.

He smiled and flutters erupted in her belly, overtaking the fire in her arm. She turned her head away. She couldn't risk getting close to this Wolf boy. No matter what the flutters in her stomach did to her. Not even if he was her mate.

Her love could kill him, might have already condemned him. He'd refused to leave her alone and that might have sealed his fate, but she wasn't going to compound the situation. Things were bad enough, and if she happened to get over this illness, she had to go back and save her tribe.

"We need to get moving." Gee stood, his shadowed form looming over them.

His angular face, licked by light from the torch, told stories of a long life—one that looked like it hadn't been easy. She tried to sit, but her weak body would only allow her to prop on her elbow.

"Where are we going?" She wiped her mouth. Her once-strong voice sounded so...vulnerable. So sick. She hated weakness—this was not how she wanted to be seen by anyone.

"To Wen's cabin. She's a healer I know. Best in these parts."

"Will she be able to make me better?"

"I know she can help with the pain, but I have no idea about curing you. I hope she can." Gee bent to pick her up. "Now, you be a good girl and try to rest. Try not to worry. We'll be at Wen's cabin in under an hour if we hurry. Come on, Nika, put the torch out and let's get moving."

Pain flashed up her arm and into her head. "It hurts so much."

"Soon, little butterfly, soon you'll have relief." Gee repositioned her weight closer to his chest. "I promise."

She squirmed to get comfortable in Gee's grip. How did he know her name meant butterfly? He must speak her tribal language, but how? She'd ask him when she could focus. The pain in her arm had grown constant again, with occasional shoots and sparks of more intensity. She settled in with her face pressed against Gee's chest, his arms beneath her back and knees.

"Okay, I put the torch out in the stream. Let's go," Nika said.

She felt Gee nod then the jolt of movement. He trudged through the forest—how could he not be tired after the distance they'd traveled? And why didn't he change into his bear form? He'd be able to move faster if he did. Maybe he didn't think she could hold on to his back.

He was right. Pain scorched her arm, and she tensed until the burn passed. Yes, he was right.

Or maybe he was trying to hide his shifter ability. But why? No, somehow she realized Gee knew exactly what he was doing and why.

Her stomach gurgled. When had she last eaten? She'd managed to hide her trail bag under a pile of leaves before she collapsed in the woods earlier and hadn't thought to tell them to grab the bag before they left. With the Alpha spearing her with his gaze, and the other big scary Wolf man one step from putting her out of her misery, she'd forgotten about her bag and it was too late to go back. Surely the healer would give her food.

"Is she asleep?" Nika asked.

She feigned a soft snore.

"I think so." Gee pulled her closer.

"Why hasn't she shifted to heal?" Nika whispered.

"I think this is a Wolf sickness," Gee said. "So

shifting might accelerate the spread of the disease. Maybe she knows and isn't chancing making things worse than they are."

She pondered. Her father had suggested she run north as Wolf since she'd make better time. But after a day and night of running, her forearm had almost lamed her, and she'd morphed to her human form so she could keep the weight off her injury. Sometimes being two-legged was the best thing. Not often, but sometimes.

What Gee said could be true. Being in Wolf form would possibly make the sickness worse and might have been why the open sore had gotten so bad so fast. The explanation made sense.

"Where did she come from? We found her so far from any other town...."

"I have a feeling she is from somewhere far, far from us, Nika."

"But how did she get into our woods?"

Their woods? She clenched her hands. This land belonged to her people. Before the white man came. The Americans, they called themselves. They'd made her father sign a treaty and move off ceremonial lands, and now her people lived in disease and poverty with little of their past dignity and independence. When the treaty was proposed, some had called for a Wolf uprising, but her father, the peacemaker, said no.

Don't start another war we can't win. We'll have to be sly and plan. Then, we'll attack.

"I don't know how she got here." Gee pulled her tight then sped up. "But, the fact remains, she's here. And we need to help her."

"I think it's time to get some answers," Nika said. "Let's wake her."

She strained to hear every word. So, what did he mean by "our woods"? Were he and Gee American? Who'd heard of American Wolf men and Bear men? Their clothing was different, but their faces were both brown, similar to her own. They spoke English. She'd learned the language because her father wanted her to be able to communicate with anyone. Few in her tribe had the fortune of learning. Maybe he and Gee were revered, or wealthy. Confusion made her head swim. Too many questions amidst all the pain.

"No, let her sleep. We'll wake her and find out everything we need to know when we get to the healer's cabin."

Yes, let me sleep. I'm so tired....

"I hope we'll be there soon. I want to know all about this she-Wolf you say is my mate."

And I need to know more. But I'm a patient Wolf. And I certainly am not anyone's mate.

Chapter Three

Nika crossed his arms. He wanted to check on the she-Wolf himself, but the healer wouldn't let him get any closer to the couch where she lay. He was poised to protest when Gee frowned at him, his gaze saying *let the healer do her job.*

He was the one who'd found her, why couldn't he be the one helping her? Nika scowled. How was anyone expected to learn responsibilities when people kept taking them away? Right then, he wanted to be beside her, comforting her.

The old woman puttered over Kimi's arm, mumbling and bobbing her head while she inspected the sore. The silver streaks in Wen's long, black braid shone in the lamplight, and her skin, thin as onionskin, stretched over her gnarled hands like taut rubber gloves. By Gee's account, Kimi needed serious medical attention, and Wen certainly knew what she was doing. She looked old to be a doctor. He shot Gee a stern look, but the Werebear was rapt watching the healer's ministrations and didn't turn to meet his gaze.

Wen had flown into the room in her raven form, a silver streak of feathers on her head, cawing and flapping before alighting on the floor. She'd shifted in a flash, though that was the last time she'd moved quickly. While an old woman, she moved like a glacier. He smirked.

The small hut, littered with implements of Chinese medicine, was dank and dusty. He wrinkled his nose. Shelves lined every wall except one, and every inch of space on that wall held either taxidermy or a framed painting of an animal. Books, tincture bottles, small boxes of unknown contents, and even animal bones filled the floor-to-ceiling shelves to the point that moving one thing would likely cause an avalanche of junk to crash to the floor. A long, curved tusk jutted from over the doorway to the kitchen, and perched on the thing sat a mummified monkey, holding out his paw like he was asking for more cake.

Was Wen a veterinarian or a people doctor? A taxidermist or a surgeon? The place gave him the creeps.

"Is she about done?" he asked.

Gee raised his finger to his lips. "Shh."

Nika tapped his foot. He bit back a cold shudder at the realization he might be infected, too. *I'm too young to die. I can't die now.*

Wen cleared her throat.

"What?" Gee had to bend over to stand in the small cabin, and the oil lights sent his shadow climbing the walls.

"What's wrong with her?" He moved closer.

"Wait a minute." Wen waved them off. "I need to be positive."

The older woman, bowed double in her upper back, shuffled to the far edge of the couch, and encouraged Kimi to sit upright. She did, her long hair curtaining her contorted face. So much pain. A sheen of sweat prickled her face and dark circles traced her eyes, but she didn't cry out.

Gee sighed and plunked into the only chair in the tiny living room area. Nika started to pace, then realized the cabin was too small for pacing to be effective. Claustrophobia tightened his chest and raised his Wolf hackles.

I might die. Kimi might die. I can't keep waiting. The suffocating thoughts pressed in on him, and he closed his eyes to stave off the feelings of helplessness.

Mate. He needed a good, long run through the hills—out in the fresh open air and under a wide, black sky where plants and sickness and death would fly away like dandelion seeds on the wind. He had to get the she-Wolf, his so-called mate, off his mind.

Kimi let out a gasp, and he opened his eyes. Wen prodded the area around the sore, and she threw her head back. Tears ran down her face.

"You're hurting her!" He started toward Kimi, and Gee grabbed his arm.

"Let Wen work." The Bear gripped him hard. "She has the healing magic."

He tugged, and Gee held tighter.

"But—"

"Nika!" The warning in Gee's tone hit him like a slap in the face.

"I'm sorry." He stopped and the Bear released him.

"I'm going to bandage her arm. Keep her wound from getting infected, at least."

"What's wrong with her?" Gee asked. "Do you know?"

"Let me get her cleaned up and then we'll talk." Wen trotted to one of the shelves and removed a box. She pulled out a long bandage and some ointment. "Will only take a minute."

What the ever-loving hell? Why doesn't the healer spit the truth out? He sighed. If he didn't get some answers soon, he was going to howl in a manner the old woman had never heard before. Then he was going to take her and head for a real doctor.

She looked at him, and, for an instant, their gazes met. Fluid warmth flooded him from his head to his toes and he ached to howl, to hold her and never let her go.

He looked away.

The healer sighed. She shook her head as she finished bandaging Kimi's arm. "I can't believe what I'm seeing, Gee. I never thought I'd ever—"

"What?" He clutched his shirt hem. "Will she be okay?"

Wen helped Kimi lie back on the couch. "I don't

know."

Gee stood and motioned for the older woman to sit in his vacated chair. She slumped, mouth open and long braid swinging when she bobbed.

"The *sugmanitu hota wo.*" Gee snarled.

"I'm afraid so." She twisted her fingers in her palms then rubbed her face. "At least that's what it seems to be. I've never seen the disease before in person."

"What?" He clenched his fists.

"Gray Wolf sickness," Gee said. "Hasn't been seen in these hills in ages. I'd hoped the sickness was eradicated for good."

"That doesn't sound...." He swallowed hard.

"Very bad." Wen stared across the room, focus unfixed. "No cases we know of since...well, in a very long time. Many, many generations. My great-grandmother's grandmother's grandmother wrote of the Wolf Disease. The flock knew of the devastation on the Wolf population. Our friends."

Kimi murmured, and they all turned to look at her. She stared into space, her eyes glassy and her face flushed. The shadows cast by oil light fanned over her, giving her the appearance of a rosy gargoyle.

Wen struggled to stand, grasping the chair for balance. "Okay, dear one. Let me get you some medicine for the pain, and some dinner. Then, you will rest while we figure out what we can do to help you." She tottered out through the door into the other part of the cabin.

He moved to stand beside Kimi. He wanted to hold her hand. "What's the cure?"

Gee stared at the wooden floor, shaking his head.

Nausea overtook him, and he bit back the acid filling his throat. "You're telling me there's *no* cure?"

Gee shook his head. "I'm so sorry."

Wen came through the door, carrying a glass of water and a pill.

"I refuse to believe that!" He turned to the healer. "Tell me all you know about this sickness. I've got to find a way to make her better."

Kimi mumbled, "Hot water. *Mni kȟáta.*"

"What's she talking about?"

"Here, dear, take this." Wen put the pill in Kimi's mouth then held the glass to her lips. "Drink. This will help with the pain."

Kimi swallowed the medicine. "*Mni kȟáta.*"

"Why does she keep saying that?" He looked to Gee. "I don't understand."

He'd known her less than a day, but something inside, deeper than his Wolf, told him he couldn't lose her. Gee had always been the one with all the answers. Why wasn't he fixing this problem? Why wasn't he saving Kimi?

"Water!" The healer's eyes lit up. "Let me check something." She headed to the shelf of books by the doorway and began picking through them.

"Nika, you know this means you may be infected, too." Gee sat on the floor. "And that means you can't come back to Los Lobos unless you're cleared."

He nodded. "I know. What about Ryker and Drew? And you?"

"I'm not a Wolf, so the disease won't affect me. But the others.... We may have to quarantine." Gee sighed. "They're not going to like that restriction."

"I'll fix it." Nika rubbed his hands together. He'd find a way to heal her and save the pack. Then Drew would be proud of him. And Gee would be, too.

"I don't think it's fixable." Gee's wide shoulders slumped. "But for your sake, and the pack's, I hope you're able to."

"I'll find a way. Whatever it takes."

Gee smiled. "You've always been optimistic. I hope you're right."

"Well, how was this cured before? They must've found a way to treat the illness."

Gee shrugged. "I always assumed the disease ran its course then faded into dormancy."

The healer sat in the chair and opened a heavy book on her lap. "I think I know the answer. This book has been handed down through my family for many generations. I think there's information in here on the Gray Wolf sickness." She flipped pages and ran her finger over the text, mouthing words while she read.

"I hope so." He sat beside Gee and rocked, trying to be patient. Gee trusted the woman, so he must, too. And he'd prove him wrong. There had to be a cure. He'd save Kimi and he'd save the pack.

Kimi snored lightly. He watched her breathe and then got up to cover her with the light blanket spread across the couch, tucking in the edges. "You'll be okay," he whispered. "I won't let you die."

"Mmmm." The healer leaned forward to examine a page. "Here. *He Sapa.* In the Black Hills where the hot springs bubble from the ground and the *mako hloke tate*, the Cave of Wind, blows, grows a wahca, flower, to heal *sugmanitu hota wo*."

"That's easy," he said. "I know that place. Let's go to the Wind Caves and pick the flowers. We can be back by daybreak."

"Hold on." Gee stretched his legs in front of him and pushed his long braid behind his shoulder. "I have a feeling this is no ordinary flower."

"You'd be right," the healer said. "The picture shows genus *Saxifrage*, but this variety has been extinct for a very long time. Look."

She held the book out to Gee, and he nodded. Nika looked at the drawing. The flower appeared the same as a thousand others spread over the plains and forests.

"Won't another variety work?" Nika asked. "We have dozens of species growing around here."

The healer shook her head. "This one, with tiny purple flowers marked with a deep-blue center, is the only one that will work." She closed the book. "They used to grow by the hot springs. That's why she keeps repeating 'hot water.' She was trying to get to the springs."

"How do you know another flower in the same family won't work? We have to try something." He ran his hands through his curls. Why was everyone sitting around pondering what to do when they should be moving?

"I'm sorry, Nika." Wen set the book on the tiny table. "The plant is extinct. My family's record is clear. This is the only variety that will work. In the last plague, my family gathered these flowers in their beaks and dropped them to the Wolf pack. This time, it isn't possible. The only flower that will cure the disease no longer grows in the Black Hills, or anywhere else on earth."

"But maybe they're wrong."

"Nika...." Gee warned. "Don't shoot the messenger."

"But there has to be a way!"

Wen rubbed her hands. "We'd need enough to make tea for everyone exposed, and she may need more than one dose since she is so ill. A lot of extinct flowers."

He held his tongue. He shouldn't be rude to Wen, but some other flower of the many varieties would work. Right? They should've taken her to a real hospital—maybe someone had synthesized a medicine that would work.

She groaned in her sleep, and Nika's heart lurched. He had to save her.

"We can't let her die!" He clenched his hands into fists and held his Wolf back. Shifting now, when he was upset, would make him look like a youth with no control. Gee would be disappointed. But his Wolf clamored to come out, to run, to fix things.

Gee and the healer looked into each other's eyes and hidden conversation passed without an uttered word. Gee gave a slight nod.

"I think we can help you find the plant," Wen whispered. "But the journey's going to be very risky and you may not survive. You're going to have to go back to a time when the flowers thrived in the Black Hills."

***

"Time travel? You've got to be kidding." Nika paced in front of the small hole in the rock. A steady current of cool air blew from the dark underground cave and he shivered.

A few lights twinkled on the ridge above him, and Gee's small lantern cast a yellow glow over the area, illuminating the grass carpeting and the dark woods like a fairy wonderland. Kimi had been asleep since the healer gave her pain medication, and Gee had set her on the soft ground near the cave vent.

Gee looked at Wen and smiled.

"Well?" he asked. "You *are* kidding, right? All the stories on the drive here are some big set up. You're punking me because I screwed up my first scouting mission, right?"

The long piercing call of an owl bored through the dense woods, and his Wolf perked up.

Shift.

No, he had to carry out the plan. No time for hunting or play. At least she wasn't in pain, thanks to the medicine. If she knew the scheme Gee and Wen had concocted, she'd think they were all crazy, though if Gee was right, maybe she knew more about things than he did.

Maybe they were all crazy.

"No. Not kidding." Gee cocked his head to listen to the night sounds. "But we've got to hurry. If the humans find us out here, we'll have to answer questions we aren't prepared for."

The healer leaned on her gnarled willow cane with the embedded glass eyeball wrapped with leather strands holding raven feathers. She stared at the hole in the rock face, letting the wind blow her braided hair back. She took a long, slow breath.

They'd passed the sign for Wind Cave National Park, then Gee had led them around the mountain to an out of the way area where a small hole allowed the wind to escape the underground, away from the main touristy site and cavern entrance. The expansive cave twisted and turned inside the rock face like a thousand ant tunnels winding through the dark with few small openings to the outside world. The opening they stood in front of would barely allow a small squirrel to pass through.

"I can't believe I'm agreeing to this," he said. "I guess the worst thing that can happen is none of this will work and we have to resort to a hospital."

"You've got to trust in things you can't see," Gee said.

They'd had to hike into the woods from Wen's cabin then Gee borrowed a car from someone on a nearby farm—it'd still taken them a couple hours to get to the cave site. Nika had slept in the car, and now he was refreshed and his senses alert.

"Yes, this is the place." Wen turned, her aged face bathed in the yellow light from the lantern. "It's time."

"Okay." He put his hands on his hips. "I'm having a hard time believing all this. No way people or even Wolf-shifters can time travel. Not possible." Why had he allowed them to talk him into dragging her to the park in the first place? She should be in a hospital. One that didn't require extinct flowers for a cure. Maybe Wen had drugged him, too. But on the way to the cave, she and Gee spoke about time travel as if it happened every day. All the talk of saber-toothed tigers and bears and dire wolves while they hiked didn't help at all—it added to the madness.

"Where do you think Kimi came from?" Gee asked.

"What do you mean?"

"How did she turn up outside Los Lobos without anyone realizing? Look at her leather slippers and her homespun dress. Those aren't modern. Either she traveled forward in time by accident, or her people helped her. Hoping for a cure—the hot water. Maybe they thought the future held a cure for her."

"Just because she acts like she's from another time doesn't mean she is." Nika blew a curl out of his face. He was going to wake up soon from the most bizarre dream he'd ever had. None of this could be real. He was used to obeying Gee, though this was getting ridiculous.

"Don't you think she deserves a chance to be cured? And what about you? You said you'd handle this. Find the cure." Gee patted him on the back. "Have a little faith in the old ways. You don't know everything, pup."

Nika's hackles rose, but he remained quiet. Not many things annoyed Gee, but the conversation appeared to be straining the Bear's patience. He closed his eyes. At least he was with Kimi.

The healer took out a packet of fragrant herbs and sprinkled them on the ground in a circle, chanting in a language he didn't recognize.

"Fine. I'm not saying I believe you, but I'm willing to try this ceremony." He kneeled beside Kimi. "Anything to help her. And to help the pack."

"Remember, lots of flowers. Good thing it's late summer when they will be blooming. If we had this problem in January, we'd be out of luck." The healer handed him a drawstring canvas sack. "You may not get the chance to go back, so fill this with as much of the *saxifrage* as you can. Remember, only the purple blooms with a blue center."

"Got it." He folded the sack and stuck it in his small backpack. Gee had outfitted him with a little food and fire-making supplies to make the tea, plus some more pain medication. "What if we can't figure out how to get back?" His heart thudded, and he reached for Kimi's hand, her fingers hot and unmoving in his grasp. "What if we get stuck there? If we get there in the first place."

"It's why she's traveling with you. In case you can't return. At least you'll be together." Wen looked up to the sky. "A falling star. A good omen. Travel safely, little Wolves."

Gee clasped him on the shoulder. "You'll get back. I don't know how, but I feel it."

"I hope you're right." *He'd better be.* He took a deep breath and scanned the area, all dark outside the small circle of lantern light and the starry Milky Way stippling its way across the sky. "Will you wait for us?"

"I'll stay near here," Gee said. "Wen will go to the car and wait. I'll let Drew know, and he can send someone to retrieve her. Don't worry about us. Right now, you need to focus on your task. We'll handle things here."

"Okay." He took a deep breath. "This all sounds so crazy."

"No crazier than a man shifting into a wolf or bear. Imagine how many people in the world think that's an impossibility. Yet, we know it's true."

"You're right. But I'm still nervous."

Gee smiled. "I'd be worried if you weren't a little scared. If anyone can handle this, it's you."

Pride filled him. "Thanks, Gee. I'll do my best."

"Are you ready?" Wen asked.

He nodded and squeezed Kimi's hand. He ran his finger down her soft cheek. He had to protect her. Save her. *I hope this works.*

"Don't delay." Gee pulled a long-sheathed knife out of the side of his boot. "And take this. In the past, everything you meet is a potential enemy. Be careful. Remember what we talked about. The animals are dangerous, and so are many of the plants. Get the flowers then get back here."

He swallowed hard and took the weapon. "Let's do this." He slipped the blade into his pack.

Gee and the healer backed away, and he closed his eyes and waited, clasping Kimi's hand as tight as he dared. If the cave held magic, then now was the time to see what it could do. The healer chanted from somewhere at the edge of the clearing, and then the wind picked up, swirling not only around Nika and Kimi, but through his closed eyes in a burst of purple and silver, alongside his spine, his Wolf, and into his heart.

Chapter Four

Kimi squinted against the bright sunlight, and then slammed her eyes shut. When had the sun come up? The ground was hard beneath her. Was she still by the creek? Was the whole evening nothing more than a dream? She winced as pain shot up her arm and stabbed her in the heart. Wherever she was, the illness was real and getting worse.

She moaned and rolled to the side. No, it couldn't be a dream. The last thing she remembered was laying on Wen's couch, listening to her talk about the Gray Wolf sickness. Wen had given her medicine for pain, and Nika had comforted her.

Nika.

"Nika...." she rasped.

"I'm here." A warm hand slid into hers, sending

tingles up her good arm. "Are you okay?"

"What happened?" She opened her eyes again and tried to sit up. "Where are we?"

He steadied her, holding her back. "You won't believe this. I'm not sure I do either."

When the world around her came into focus, her heart sped. Large trees resembling pines towered over her, and an overgrowth of tangled ferns carpeted the ground in the shadows. The aroma of wildflowers and dirt played on the warm air, and when she turned her head, the wind blew her hair about her face. She examined the hole in the rocky hillside.

A cave.

"The Cave of Winds?" She brushed a lock of hair from her face.

"Yes." He touched her cheek then pushed her hair behind her ear. "But there's something else."

A giant dragonfly danced by, its iridescent wings buzzing with exertion. She'd never seen an insect so large—the wingspan was the length of her arm.

She swallowed down the panic rising in her throat. She remembered. The talk of time travel and going into the far past to find the ingredient for the cure to her sickness. "What else?" she whispered, her swirling vision threatening to overwhelm her into a whirlpool of sensation. She had to hear him say the words.

"We're in the past." He rubbed her hand with his thumb. "The very distant past."

"Yes." She examined the cave entrance. Not huge, but big enough for a person to squeeze into. The Cave of Winds was sacred to her people, and she was near the hot springs her father told her to travel to. The cool air blowing from the cave chilled her, and she shivered.

"You know we're in the past?" He slid closer, his hip brushing hers and sending little jolts of pleasure to her core. "And you believe it?"

"Yes, I do. I heard the healer, Wen, talk about what we need to do." She leaned into him. "Find a flower. A purple one with a blue center." Maybe this was a dream and she was laying on some shaman's pallet in her father's tipi in a delirium. But he was a real man, not a dream creature. Hard in all the right places. She caught his gaze and dipped her head. Yes, he was as she remembered, all real. "That will be the cure to my illness. Guess we should find it."

He smiled and flutters raced through her belly.

She smiled back.

"We do need to hurry. We don't want to be stuck here any longer than we have to be." He pulled the knife from his pack. "And Gee warned this place could be dangerous. From the size of the insects, I believe him. He warned me they'd be bigger, but I had no idea they'd be *so* huge."

An unknown bird shrieked under the tree canopy, its shrill call echoing through the dense forest.

"Then let's find the flower and go." She took a deep breath. If this was her only chance, she'd take it.

"Can you walk?" He scanned the edge of the forest. "We have to head toward the hot springs, but they aren't far. Wen said we'd find the flowers growing around the pools."

"I think so." She looked up to the tops of the tall trees towering high and blocking all but a bit of warm sunshine. Long masses of moss draped the tallest branches, and deep-purple vines crisscrossed the forest's treetops.

Inside, her Wolf paced and whined, and Kimi quieted her. "My arm hurts, but I don't feel dizzy anymore." She picked at the bandage Wen had placed on her sore. It was stained with dirt.

Nika smiled. "I'm glad. Wen gave you pain medication last night. I have more if you need some."

"No, I'm all right. I feel much better than I did." She tried to stand, her legs weak and wobbly and her knees coming close to giving way.

He caught her before she hit the ground, his arms strong and warm around her back. He pulled her against his chest, hesitating before speaking. "Are you sure you can walk?" he whispered.

She looked down and pulled away. He was so close.

Too close?

Her Wolf panted to be released, whining, wanting to run with her mate through the ancient forest.

Mate? Yes, that feels right. But I don't even know him. And my father won't approve.

"Help me stand." Kimi's Wolf had once run free at her slightest nod, but since she'd been sick, her Wolf had been trapped. She shuddered.

Now she'd found her mate in some future she couldn't have dreamed of and had traveled with him to someone else's past. Everyone's past. Too much to contemplate.

He pulled her up and set her on her feet. He didn't let go. He rubbed her lower back with gentle firm strokes. "You sure you're okay to walk? I don't want to leave you here alone; it's too dangerous. I can carry you if needed."

"Yes, I can walk. But not fast." She braced herself. She was not a weak female. If she could reveal her Wolf, he'd believe. Until then, she'd have to prove it to him in human form. What if the illness had progressed to the point where it affected her ability to change at all? Her Wolf whimpered. Didn't matter. Things would be okay. She'd get better, and she'd show him her strong Wolf—she wasn't the weakling the illness made her out to be. How she hated it. She'd get well, and they'd run in the moonlight.

Together.

She focused on moving one foot ahead, and keeping her balance even though her vision teetered along its own periphery. She put her arms out to steady herself. Too bad she was sick. This verdant forest with strange twisted trees and lush, wiry undergrowth would be heaven to explore.

He smiled. "Lean on me if you have to."

She nodded. Maybe leaning on him was a good idea after all. She could conserve the little strength she had, just in case. She snaked her hand underneath his arm, savoring the electric charge shooting through her as their skin touched.

"We'll go slowly." He took a step.

"Okay." She crept forward, matching him a step at a time, their footsteps crackling through leaves and ferns.

A large bird squawked over them, and she peered up to watch the bird circle. Wings spread, the black bird commanded the sky above the pines. Another bird appeared over the treetops, and the birds pirouetted and dove in an aerial mating dance. Her face flushed, and she stole a peek at him.

He leaned close, his breath teasing her face. "Beautiful, isn't it? So free."

She nodded and closed her eyes, savoring his soft touch as he rubbed alongside her jaw, and then the warm press of his lips on hers. Soft, then harder. His tongue flicked out over her lips then was gone, replaced by his lips once again, lingering for a few unsure moments.

For a fleeting second, they bonded when her Wolf howled and her heart thundered as if awakened for the first time.

Then he pulled away.

"We'd better go," he whispered.

Her Wolf panted. She opened her eyes and touched her lips. Yes, he'd kissed her. Gently, softly, perfectly. In that moment, nothing else mattered. Not death, not danger, not illness. Not even the thought both her pack and his could be sick now. Only Nika mattered.

Mate.

They'd save the world tomorrow.

He smiled. "We'd better go," he repeated. "Let's pick these flowers and get home."

With the kiss lingering on her lips and the hope of more to come, she followed, oblivious to the pain and their predicament. Of course, they had to get home, and they would. For now, being near her mate filled her with a warmth she hadn't felt before. When he was near, she was more alive, more safe, more everything.

Lush, deep-green vegetation spread out before them, and they maneuvered along a narrow dirt path that must have been forged by animals heading to the water source. Years of tracking prey had taught her the best hunting grounds were those leading to water sources. Trees of every kind—many she'd never seen before—spread over them, chopping the sunbeams into thin shafts of light shooting down to the forest floor like golden daggers. Whatever this place was, whenever, didn't matter. The forest, the hills, the very air thrummed with the energy of her ancestors. Maybe she and Nika had stumbled through the veil into the spirit world, crossing the delicate boundary between the living and the dead. Wherever they were, was right. She belonged with this man Wolf, now, in this time she'd never visited.

My mate. Her Wolf bayed in agreement.

He supported her, and she kept her feet moving. Step by step, they'd get to the hot water and the flowers Wen said they needed. A loud squall echoed through the forest, silencing the insects. He pulled her along faster.

"What was that?" she asked.

"I don't know, but it didn't sound happy. We'd better try to pick up the pace a bit."

They walked on a few minutes, with no more

noise coming from the deep forest. She took a deep breath. "It's gone now," she said.

"Let's hope so. We don't want to deal with the animals that live in these woods."

She nodded. His brave front was just that—a front. She sensed his fear, and he likely sensed hers. This forest was dangerous, and there was no one around to help them if they came across trouble, yet they walked arm-in-arm. Emotion took over and eased the reality of their situation.

"So, your name means butterfly?" He ducked to go under a low-hanging branch.

"Yes. My father named me. My full name is Kimimela."

"Beautiful. And fitting."

She blushed. "Thank you. What is the meaning of your name?"

He laughed. "Nika means victory. Supposedly. But I can't say I've been victorious in a long time."

"A strong name. You'll live up to it." They paused to step through a tangle of ferns. "Where are your parents?" She took in a quick breath, regretting she'd asked.

"My parents." His grip tensed on her arm. "Long

dead. I don't speak of them often, since they abandoned me. I was raised by others in the pack. An orphan, pretty much."

They climbed over a large fallen tree lying across the path, Nika helping her over the knobby bark and down onto the other side where the tiny path resumed. Good thing he knew where he was going. Gee and Wen must have told him how to get to the hot springs.

"I'm so sorry." She panted. How much longer could she walk? Her arm stung, and her heart raced. Her legs were so weak. "Being raised by someone other than your father and mother must've been hard on you."

"Not really. If they didn't want me, why would I want them? Besides, there's no point in worrying over it now. It's done." He pulled her forward.

"I suppose. But it's still sad."

He shrugged. "What about you? Where are your parents?"

She took a deep breath. She should've known he'd ask. "My mother died during a long childbirth with me. Three days she lay in agony, waiting on me to be born. I was born as life passed from her to the sky, so I sometimes walk with the dead at my side. My father says it's what gives me the ability to move through worlds." A sharp pain shot up her arm, and she dropped to her knees, holding her arm.

"What's wrong?" He knelt beside her. "It's hurting a lot?"

She blinked away the tears. "I can tolerate the pain."

He pulled her up. "Can I get you more medicine?"

"No. It'll make me sleep, and you can't carry me all the way to the springs. I'll be all right."

She winced at the burning in her arm. By the spirits, she hoped this flower healed her quickly. So many days in pain. She was wearing down.

"We don't have much farther to go." He coaxed her along. "Now, finish telling me about your spirit walking."

"Are you teasing me?" She searched his face for any hint he was, but found none. Memories of other girls in her tribe picking on her over her tales flooded her. Even though her father was chief, she hadn't been able to escape the cruelty of being perceived different. Odd. The spirit girl—one who would never have a mate.

"No. I think it's interesting. I've never known anyone with that kind of ability. I didn't know it even existed."

They moved through a low-hanging area of the forest, the branches and leaves bowing down and kissing the forest floor. The smell of mud and minerals swirled through the moist air.

They were nearing the hot springs, thank the spirits.

"Well, I haven't experienced travel through real time until Father and his shaman sent me to your woods. Before I got sick, I dream walked at night. Speaking to my mother. Seeing ancestors lining the waterfront, bodies stacked like a stone dam...."

"Umm. Okay. Those are some wild visions." He stopped. "I guess that's why you believed Wen about our travel into the past. I'll admit I was skeptical of what she said. But this"—he motioned to the forest around him—"isn't similar to any forest I know of. And I trust Gee. He doesn't lie."

"He's a bear?"

He nodded. "A big one."

She laughed. *Yes, he was.* Being around Nika,

even in the current circumstances, made her happy. Made her Wolf happy. "By the way, your Wolf is beautiful. He took my breath away, even though I tried to get you to leave. I didn't want you to get sick."

He blushed and pushed curls out of his face. "Thank you. I knew you were Wolf, too, when I scented you."

He knew. "Yes. But I can't change now, at least not like I could before. I wouldn't want to risk shifting, even if I could. Since I got so sick, I can't make it happen." She winced again as pain tore through her battered arm and up into her shoulder. She coughed, sending the shooting pains throughout her chest. The sickness was spreading.

"That's horrible!" He stopped and held her hands. "I don't know if I could handle not being able to shift."

"I'm managing."

"I promise, I will help you get well. You'll get your Wolf back."

"Thank you."

"I mean it, Kimi. Whatever it takes, I'm going to fix this."

"I know you will." She squeezed his hands. He

understood. No Wolf would want to lose shifting abilities. "There's something else."

"What?"

"My tribe is unwell. Many have died, and many more are sick. I have to get better and take the knowledge of healing back to my tribe and save them." Even though every bone in her body rebelled at the idea, she accepted her duty.

"We'll find the flower. Heal everyone. So stop worrying." He brushed her hair aside with his fingertips.

"We'll do this together."

"Yes, we will. And even though this is a terrible situation, I found you. Fate, butterfly."

She tipped her head up, and he lowered his mouth to hers, sending explosions of color through her body as his tongue searched hers.

Her Wolf howled.

Chapter Five

Nika searched the fringes of the deep woods while they walked, alert to any movement or potentially dangerous shadow. Foreboding crept up his spine and settled in the back of his head. He sensed the danger, no matter how pretty the scenery was. Dirt, decomposing leaves, and rotting fruit scented the air. With Kimi beside him, he was on hyper alert. He wouldn't let anything happen to her.

And what the heck had he been thinking when he kissed her? He'd kissed her not once, but twice, letting his guard down in what could be the most dangerous forest he'd ever see. Trees as tall as skyscrapers blocked most of the sunlight, creating a shadow land where monsters could dwell. Did dwell. And he was making out with a girl. Some scout he was. Gee and Drew would push him back into training if they knew how he'd acted. He was supposed to be protecting her, and all he wanted to do was lay her on the ground and claim her.

Over and over again.

Was it anything more than instinct? Could it be, when he'd just met her?

She leaned on him, her gait unsteady. If only she really were a butterfly with heavy wings that could take them to the end of the journey. He smiled and hugged her to him.

"I'm tired." She stopped walking.

"Come on," he said. "You can do this. A little farther."

He'd enjoyed kissing her, no mistake there. He'd enjoyed kissing too much, truth be told. But his timing wasn't the best. What if she thought he was taking advantage of her? She was sick and dying, and he kissed her. She'd kissed back, but she was near delirious. He sighed. Scout, guide, helper...he failed at all of them. Would he ever have the confidence Drew had? Or the toughness of Ryker? Or would he forever be the one stepping in trouble and second-guessing everything, never growing up? The universe mocked him when he'd been given his name. He no more represented victory than a river rock represented a diamond.

A stab of pain pierced his thigh, and he lost his footing, tumbling to the ground. His thigh burned, and he put pressure on the painful place.

"What happened?" She bent over him.

"Must be a muscle cramp," He said through clenched teeth. But the pain wasn't. He knew what was happening but he wasn't going to worry her.

He was infected.

"You better drink more water." She held her hand out to help him up.

"I will." He took her outstretched hand and stood. The pain had dimmed to a faint buzz. He had time. They'd get the flowers and both would be well before she even knew he was sick. "Let's hurry."

Up ahead, the forest thinned and opened into a bright meadow with slender grass waving across the surface like ripples on the sea. Yellow flowers flickered at the tops of long stems, bowing and bobbing in the light breeze. The thick odor of mineral-rich mud filled the air as they approached the clearing and the heat of the day crept into the dark, cool forest edge.

He motioned her to be quiet and pulled her to the side, off the tiny path.

"Let me get a good look at this meadow before we head in," he whispered. "See if the area's safe. There's nowhere to hide, and it's a perfect place to be ambushed." His Wolf paced, begging to be set free. Dare he? The illness would accelerate if he did. But he could cover the area faster if he shifted.

She nodded, her deep-brown eyes wide. What he wouldn't give to be able to spend the day kissing her soft mouth. He ran his fingertip along her jaw, and she shivered.

Mate.

He shook his head to clear the thoughts. *Focus.*

She folded her hands and stepped back.

"I'm going to change so I can cover more ground in a short time."

"Go ahead."

Her firm acknowledgment strengthened him, and he took a deep breath. His Wolf surged at his mate's acceptance. "Be right back. Stay here and keep still. Don't draw any attention to yourself. Scream if you need me." He dropped to the ground and ran, the pads of his paws skimming the earth as he scouted the perimeter of the meadow. Smells of dirt and leaves and grass swirled through the air, somehow stronger and richer than his own world. *Dirtier and healthier*. The afternoon sun warmed him to his core, and he yipped like a puppy. He was safe here—no scary creatures. Only a virgin world waiting on exploration. *Freedom*. Flowers tickled his jowls when he leapt, their pungent odor wild and untamed. *I feel alive!*

He circled to check the same area again then headed to the far side of the grassy area. Warm, muggy air filled his nostrils where the meadow thinned, and he stopped to sniff. Pools of steaming green water spread out all the way to a cliff face wet with humidity. A river ran alongside the pools, bubbling and splashing over rocks and tree limbs, and another forest lay beyond with more grand mountains in the distance. He pawed at the ground.

Nirvana.

An explosion of tiny purple flowers with blue centers dotted the deep-green grass around the pools.

Saxifrage.

Delighted, he lifted his snout to howl, then

remembered. He was far from home in a dangerous world. His howl could be heard for miles, and he couldn't risk alerting something to his position. His heart thumped, and he wagged his tail. *Run!*

Nose to the ground, he trekked along the border where the meadow met the more compacted grass and the warm pools lay. A zillion bugs flew up from a decaying log, and a cloud of insects rose in the air then whisked away on an unseen current. He checked the ground again.

Footprints. He sniffed, his hackles raising and twitching. Big footprints. *Wolf.* More than one. Days-old footprints. From the size of the prints, very large wolves frequented the area, and he didn't want to be here when they returned. They might even be dire wolves. He trotted, following the prints till he lost them in the water.

Safe. For now. With one last glance, he sprinted into the meadow toward Kimi.

***

"Did you find the flowers? The springs?" Kimi leaned against a thin tree, holding her arm.

"Yes," Nika said. "Bunches of flowers. They're growing everywhere! This is going to be easy."

"I hope you're right. Anything could happen, and we're a long way from home. I don't trust things will be so easy."

"We're going to be fine. Let's go." He reached for her, steadying her.

"I wish my Wolf could run."

"I do, too." He patted her back. "Soon. We'll have the cure, and we can run together."

"Then let's hurry."

They pushed through the tall grass and sedge, sending up bursts of yellow-green pollen. The sunlight painted sparkling highlights on Kimi's jet-black hair, and the wind tossed the strands around her face. He wanted to wrap her hair around his hand and pull her to him.

Mine.

The urge to claim her rose in his throat like a strangled howl, and he concentrated to push it back. He didn't know which ached more, his heart or his dick. Gee had warned him the mating call would be stronger than anything he'd ever felt. He was right.

Soon. Once she's well. Once we're home.

She sneezed then winced.

"You okay?" He stopped and put his hands on her shoulders. "Is the pain worsening?" What a cad he was. Thinking about mating with her when she couldn't even walk much.

She wiped her eyes. "I'm okay. Let's hurry and get these flowers."

"Let me know if you need the medicine. I hate seeing you suffer."

"I will."

The willowy grass thinned when they reached the edge of the meadow. He scanned the area, on constant alert for any signs of trouble. If the wolves came back, he and Kimi would be in a world of trouble. The task would've been easier if he let his Wolf run, but she needed his help.

The hot springs had formed half a dozen small pools beside the small river, all oddly shaped with grasses and shrubs right up to the water's edge. The river meandered in a hook around the area and splashed against large rocks littering its bed. On the far side of the water, a dense forest loomed, rising on a gentle hill and going on as far as he could see.

If something bad lurked in those woods, they'd

not see the danger till it reached the river. It might be too late. He clutched Kimi. He would protect her.

"Look at all the flowers!" She straightened. "And the pools. They're beautiful."

"Let's get you settled over there." He pointed to a large boulder forming the side of one of the larger pools of warm water. "You can relax and stick your feet in the warm water while I'm collecting flowers."

"I can help you pick them."

"No, you have so little strength left." He guided her to the rock. "You rest and be lookout for me. It won't take long for me to pick enough flowers. They're everywhere."

"Okay, I guess you're right. I'm tired."

He helped her onto the warm boulder and removed her leather slippers so she could slide her feet into the green water. The sun sent rainbows across the mist rising from the warm pool.

Magical.

"Ahhh." She kicked the water, sending a shower of drops over him. "Wish we could stay here."

He laughed as the water sprinkled his face. "Wish we had time to take a dip."

"Don't we?"

"Not till I get what we came here for. After that, we'll see." In her current state, he didn't want to scare her by telling her about the wolf footprints, but there was nothing he'd rather do right now than glide into the water with her and pull her close. He set the pack down. He pulled out the sack for the flowers and started to zip the pack before reconsidering. He grabbed the knife.

"You don't think you'll need that, do you?" Her eyes were wide, and he sensed her fear.

"I hope not." He shook out the sack and bent to kiss her on the top of her head.

She smiled up at him, her fear dissipating like a dying fire and he ran his fingers through her sun-warmed hair.

"You make me feel safe."

"Oh my God!" he crouched. "Don't move."

"What?"

Words fled, and he pointed to the large mammoth on the opposite bank of the river. The bulky creature looked very little like what he'd learned in school, but the long, curved tusks and elephant build gave it away.

Holy shit, that's a big animal.

The giant pulled water into his trunk. His vibrant rust-colored wavy coat shone in the sunlight and his feet moved rhythmically, swaying as he drank.

Like elephants did at the zoo.

"Look at that behemoth," she whispered. "I've never seen such a creature. Will he eat us?" She leaned back into him, and he sensed the fear returning.

"No, I don't think so." He squeezed her shoulders. "If I remember my history lessons, this one's an herbivore. But he might charge us if he feels threatened, so let's stay still and hope he leaves."

The beast took a step back, turned, then ambled into the forest. He let out a breath of relief. He'd never seen such a strange animal, and though interesting, he didn't care to ever see one again unless it lived in a zoo.

"I'd better hurry before the rest of the herd decides to take a water break." He stood and put the bag over his shoulder.

"So big." She kicked at the water. "Glad he didn't come over on this side."

"He's gone now."

"Still, knowing the scary things that lurk in this

world.... One minute, I feel this is paradise, and the next...."

He kneeled. He cupped her face in his hand. "I won't let anything happen to you. I promise."

She nodded. "I'm tired, Nika. I want to be done with this and go home."

He brushed away a stray tear. "Let me get the flowers, so we can get out of here. I told you I'd take care of you. Let me."

"I'm acting like a child."

He shook his head. "No, you're acting like someone who's in pain and in danger. Trust me. Things are going to get better. We'll take care of your arm then your Wolf can run. I know you want that."

"Yes. I can't wait to run." She smiled. "I wish I could soak my arm in this water. I bet the warmth would feel really good."

"I don't think we can risk getting into the springs now, but when we get back home—to my time—we can. The springs are still around, though different. Safe." He set out one of the water canteens. "Drink. You need to stay hydrated."

The flower sack was close to full, and he'd picked all except a few of the flowers near the pool where

Kimi waited. Every so often, she'd wave at him and his Wolf would sing. He couldn't wait to get home to introduce her to the whole Los Lobos pack. Get a beer at Gee's Bar. Once she was healed, and the crisis averted, he knew Drew would welcome her.

He had to.

What if Kimi wants to return to her own time? She'd said she needed to take the cure back to her people. An icy spike of fear raced through him. What if she couldn't come to his time after that? He sighed. He'd have to deal with that once they were back. And if he could go with her to help her people, he would.

Anything for his mate.

He bent to pick a thatch of the low-growing flowers. He'd picked almost enough, and the sack bulged. He plucked a tiny flower and dropped the bloom into the bag. His fingers, stained purple, ached from the tedious job. How long had he been picking? At least a couple of hours, judging by the low-slung sun. The sky would soon turn orange then darken, and he didn't want to be out in the open. He didn't want to spend the night in the past either. He glanced up at her. She lay curled up on the rock, resting. Good for her to get a little rest before their trek back to the

Wind Cave.

He picked as fast as he could. A shiny rock caught his eye. He wiped away the mud and tugged the stone from the ground. A beautiful crystal of rutilated rose quartz shone in his hand. *The love stone.* Common in the Black Hills of his time. He smiled and slipped the stone into his pocket then sat back on his heels. He peeked at her on the rock, now asleep. So beautiful, like the crystal. He could lay beside her with only a few steps.

No, he had to focus on the task at hand. But he could spare one more minute enjoying the peacefulness.

This land, so full of promise, spread out in front of him like a fantasy. Nature's perfect canvas—one humans had come close to destroying in his time. What would've happened if the Black Hills had remained uninhabited? What if her people had been allowed to remain in their sacred lands? He shook his head at the loss.

History was sometimes unfortunate, especially when forgotten.

He cinched the bag and slid it onto his shoulders, hoping the flowers would be enough for Wen's needs.

He and Kimi needed to get back to the cave before nightfall.

He stood, and something big strode into the clearing, panting and half-growling.

The cat was unlike any he'd ever seen. Even his Wolf whined at the sight. Large, curved fangs, head big as a lion's, and a stocky body with huge paws.

A saber-toothed tiger.

Chapter Six

Kimi startled awake to a low, growling sound. *What's that noise?* She sat up, the throbbing in her arm rushing into her consciousness. *Where am I?* The warm water bubbling at her feet sent tendrils of thick steam into the air around her. *Mni kȟáta. The hot springs.* She glanced around. Everything was so green and bright, and the ache in her arm was so persistent, reminding her she was going to die.

The low growl rumbled through the air again. She rubbed her eyes and tried to focus. Where was the sound coming from?

Oh no!

Nika?

Bile filled her throat when she spotted him at the edge of the meadow. At least he was alive. He crouched, knife in hand, staring down the largest, and likely the most dangerous, cat she'd ever seen. The creature's mouth was open, fangs bared.

Ready to tear into her mate.

She froze, aware of her heart thumping and her inability to move. She had to help him, but all she could do was watch the battle unfold in front of her and wait her turn to be the animal's prey. If he killed Nika, she had nothing to live for anyway.

Nika took a step to the side and the cat followed, hissing and grunting. She caught a glimpse of long, sharp claws protruding from padded paws. Those claws would rip Nika apart. He wouldn't even have time to shift, not that it would matter. His Wolf would be no match for such a massive and strong creature.

Finding her muscles, she scooted back on the rock. "No!" she screamed. "Leave him alone!"

The cat turned toward her, narrowing its eyes into slits, whiskers twitching. It sniffed the air then let loose a full roar that shook her insides. She put her hands over her ears and winced at the piercing noise.

What would her father tell her to do? He'd taught

her all she knew about hunting. The number one thing was not to let yourself be seen or hunted. Always be the one with the element of surprise. Yelling hadn't been a good idea.

Now what?

If Nika ran, the cat would catch him within a stride or two. The tiger paced, paws thumping on the dusty ground. Nika clasped the blade. A breeze pushed past, tossing his curls—the only movement from his statue-still body.

Drool trailed the ground where the creature paced. Kimi wrinkled her nose.

She didn't sense the animal was a shifter. Its presence was all animal, all feral. So no reasoning, no trying to bargain.

Kill or be killed.

She had to help Nika. She scrambled over the boulder, looking for smaller rocks to throw at the beast, not caring if she drew the tiger's attention. She gathered a couple medium-sized pebbles and flung them at the tiger, wincing when hot pain ripped through her arm and chest. One bounced off its back. The animal didn't even flinch.

Its focus remained on Nika.

She threw a larger one, and the stone grazed the animal's head. The cat stopped pacing and sniffed the air, its breath coming in puffs.

"Kimi get out of here!" He crouched again, knife in hand. "Now!"

"No!" She slid off the rock, scraping her legs. "I'm not leaving you behind." Her tenuous balance crumpled, but she held onto the rock to steady herself. She pelted the animal with a larger stone, and he turned toward her, growled then hissed. Heart in throat, she backed away, willing her feet to move across the muddy grass.

With the tiger's attention on Kimi, Nika took the opportunity to land a blow between the animal's shoulder blades with his knife. The cat's back bloomed red with blood. Angry, it twisted and lunged at Nika, knocking him to the ground in one vicious pounce. The knife sailed out of his hand, clattering to the dusty ground. The tiger stood over him and let out a roar, shaking its head and slinging saliva.

Ready to finish the job.

The tiger was going to kill Nika. Rip his throat out.

Dazed, she forced her legs to move, her bare feet

pricked raw by the rocky ground. With a lunge and a painful jump, she grabbed the cat's broad back, the smell of musk mingled with her own fear assailing her nostrils. Slipping down its side, blood ran down her arms, she grasped for anything to hold to, burying her hands into the bloody fur. If only she could shift. Then she could use her teeth and her super strength. If only she weren't sick....

Where was he? No time to see how he was. One misstep and the tiger would kill her.

The tiger lurched when she pummeled the back of its head with her fist, hanging on with her good arm. The cat snapped again and again, trying to catch any part of her in its teeth, and she was somewhat aware of Nika screaming at her to run, to leave him. Smears of saliva covered her hair and dress, and she cringed at how close the tiger's teeth were getting with each try.

One bite making contact and she'd be dead.

With the tiger's forceful lunge and a ripple of back muscles, she lost her balance. She grabbed at the fur but slipped and slid off one side. Rolling across the muddy pebble-covered ground and covering her face against the attack that was coming, she prayed for the end.

This is it.

Wicate. Death.

Sounds and smells retreated, and her mind filled with lack of thought. She couldn't hear him anymore, or the sounds of the water. The odor of tangy, coppery blood filled the air, replacing all other smells. And birds. Lots of birds.

Was he dead? He must be. The cat had time to finish him, and he hadn't come to save hers. She closed her eyes and waited on the tiger's deathblow. Her body felt like the mud she lay in. Without bones, warm, and watery. Exhausted.

A long, low howl filled the air, vibrating her insides and sending chills throughout her body. The howl was followed by another one, then another, all different frequencies.

Wolves!

The tiger's breath, rancid with the stench of death, warmed her face in a series of rapid puffs then was gone. The tiger growled low and walked away.

What was happening? Was the cat going to get a running start to attack? Was it going back to Nika?

She didn't move, unable to convince her tired

muscles to cooperate. Her heart fluttered, like it didn't exist in the same earth plane she did. Had she stared down death and won? She must be in the *wanagiyata*, spirit land. When had she crossed? Maybe the tiger *had* bitten her.

She peeked.

Forming a circle around the pools were at least ten of the largest wolves she'd ever seen. Huge wolves, more massive than even her grandfather had been, and he'd been a giant among Wolves. Tails up and forelegs in a squat, the wolves were in attack position.

She and Nika couldn't win in this world filled with dangerous creatures. They'd never be able to escape so many. Death by tiger would have been better. At least life would be over.

The tiger crouched in the middle of the pack, swinging its gaze from one wolf to another, growling. Ears flat against its head, and wheezing. Though the cat was a massive animal, the wolves stood taller at their shoulders and their bulk was greater. And there were close to a dozen of them.

She sat up and pushed her hair out of her face. No one even turned to see what she was doing. All focus remained on the injured tiger. She could run into the woods if she wanted, but she would not leave him behind. He'd tried to save her from the tiger....

Where is he?

Bile filled her parched mouth when she remembered the fight.

Dead.

Nika lay on the ground, mere feet from the big cat. He wasn't moving, and his legs splayed in an odd angle.

Tears rushed her eyes, and she brushed them away. *No. He can't be dead.* They'd found each other. The *tunkasila*, Great Spirit, wouldn't be so cruel.

He moaned, and several of the large wolves turned to him. One nudged him with a nose, and he scooted back trying to get out of the way.

He's alive!

The tears turned to happy tears, and she covered her mouth with her hand to avoid screaming. Then she realized it didn't matter they were alive. No way would they escape all the wolves, even if they had a gun to shoo them away with. They weren't even a close match to the pack in front of them.

The tiger didn't pay attention to Nika—his focus

was on the circle beginning to close in. The animals bared their teeth and snapped as they came nearer. Short and stocky at the hips but longer than most, the dire wolves' appearance alone was enough to frighten all but the toughest person. Their fur, spiky and full, ranged from black to a ruddy gray, and their long torso was meant for running. No females were among the group.

Her heart throbbed in her throat. She watched them surround the tiger. They needed a plan. He stood and ran to her, stumbling through the circle without so much as a bared muzzle or growl. The wolves seemed intent on terrorizing the tiger for the moment.

"Are you okay?" He took her hand. "I can't believe you hopped on the tiger. Are you crazy?"

She nodded. "Okay for now." Her arm hurt, but with everything going on, the pain didn't seem like much of a problem compared to the tiger and the wolves.

"Okay or crazy?"

"Both?" She smiled.

"Yes." He drew her into a hug, and she went limp against him, letting his strength pour over her for a second. She wasn't a weak female, but something about letting her mate hold the burden for a moment was an intimacy she'd never allowed.

She looked over his shoulder at the circle of wolves. "What're we going to do? We can't run; they'll catch us."

"I don't know yet. I'll think of something."

"Look!" She grasped him tighter.

He turned them both so they could watch the spectacle.

One of the wolves, a large gray one peppered with black-tipped fur, lunged at the tiger, snapping at its legs in rapid fire. Before he blinked, three more jumped into the fray, one on the cat's back. The tiger hissed and growled and pawed at the air, trying to figure out which wolf to attack first. Fur flew and then spatters of blood.

She buried her face in Nika's chest. The cat was no match for the wolves, and even though the tiger would've killed both of them, she didn't relish seeing it suffer and die.

They would be next. He hugged her tight and rubbed her lower back. She clung to him, listening to his staccato heartbeat. She sensed his fear, his protection, his love, and she projected her love back to him, hoping he could feel her emotions above all the craziness around them. Nothing like death to bring people closer.

He kissed her forehead.

One last strangled scream and she opened her eyes. The cat, bloodied and ripped apart, lay dead on the ground. Two wolves trotted to the carcass and dragged it away, leaving a red trail in the dust. Tremors shook her, and she vomited. Nika murmured soothing comments and held her hair away from her face. She retched until only bile came up.

The remaining wolves padded closer, forming a loose semicircle around them.

"You know you're my mate, and I'll do anything to protect you," Nika whispered. "Whatever happens here."

"Not against this pack. Too many. You saw what they did to the cat. We can't win." She hugged him. "If we die now, at least we die together. Even though I've only known you a short time, I wouldn't ever be happy if something happened to you. I love you, Nika Wolf."

"And I love you, butterfly." He pulled her to him, and she closed her eyes and held on tight.

A voice hung heavy in the air. A voice she didn't recognize, speaking words she didn't understand, garbled and deep and resonant. She looked up to see three of them had morphed into three of the largest Native Americans she'd ever seen, and one held Nika's knife.

Chapter Seven

The Native American mumbled in his guttural language again. Nika tensed and pushed Kimi behind him where he hoped she'd at least feel somewhat safe. He could sense her fear, strong and exposed. She'd had enough for the day, and he'd make sure this new threat wouldn't make things worse, if that were even possible.

Somehow he'd protect her from the Wolves, no matter what it took. Gee had trained him well.

"Do you understand what he's saying?" Nika asked. "Is he speaking Sioux?"

He could feel her shaking her head no.

He scanned the group of men. So the massive Wolves were shifters. When he'd seen them arrive and take down the saber-tooth, from their great size he knew they were dire wolves, but he hadn't sensed any shifting powers—even with his heightened empathic ability. How they'd hidden their ability was a mystery. Maybe he hadn't been paying attention, with all the other things going on around them at the time.

"What are they going to do to us?" Kimi whispered. She squeezed his shoulders and pressed her breasts against his back. "They have your knife."

Nika strangled a moan at her softness. Would he ever get to hold her in his arms without the fear of death hanging over him? *Stay focused. They could kill us.* "Don't know, but I'm going to find out, and I'm gonna get my knife back. At least I can talk to them, unlike the tiger." *What the hell is wrong with me?*

He took a pained step toward the men, and Kimi followed. His thigh burned like a hot poker was wedged between the bone and muscle and someone was twisting the blistering iron. Her arm, in much worse shape, had to feel like it was about to fall off. Yet, he still thought about sex. He shook his head. Gee had warned him, but no amount of prep could've prepared him.

The Wolf men stood still, only their eyes tracking to follow his movements, their beards lifting in the breeze like little flags.

"You okay?" Her fingertips never left his shoulders.

"Yeah, a bit sore," he whispered. *And a lot scared.*

Gee had filled him in on most of the fauna of the time—saber-tooths, mammoths, slugs, large insects, and dire wolves. Known for their tight communities and strong jowls, he'd hoped they wouldn't run into dire wolves at all. Yet, here they were.

No telling how the creatures would react to their smaller kin—they could very well feel territorial since dire wolves ran in tight packs.

And they were predators—he could tell by their sharp Wolf teeth.

But they'd rescued him and Kimi from death, and now one of them was trying to communicate. In some other language, but still, communication was a good sign. A dire wolf was trying to talk to him, and creatures didn't talk to their food.

Why couldn't he sense any emotion? Maybe because they were from so far in the past? Were they so different?

"Hello?" He tried to look strong but not combative. He'd never be able to defend himself against even one of these Wolves. Not alone. Why didn't Gee come with him? Why hadn't Drew and Ryker or at least some of the other orphans come with him to the past to help him? Would the entire Tao pack even have a chance against these monstrous creatures?

The large man Wolf, dressed in a loincloth of what looked to be silvery red mammoth fur with a shawl of soft leather, pointed to the cat being dragged away. He made gestures of a snapping mouth and pointed to Nika then to Kimi, and then to his men.

Nika nodded and bowed his head in deference, as he should. "Thank you for saving us. We are ever in your debt." He stood straight.

Was he the Alpha? Did dire wolves even have the same pack structure as the Tao? Or was this womanless pack very different?

He held out the knife, and Nika grabbed the blade before the Wolf changed his mind.

"Thank you."

Grunt. He pointed to Kimi and Nika, then the

river.

Nika frowned. What did the he mean? There wasn't anything on the other side of the river except forest and hills. Was he trying to get them to leave?

"No." She clutched his T-shirt. "I'm not going over there. We need to go to the Wind Cave, so we can get back home."

The Wolf man gestured again, grunting and stomping.

"I don't understand." He shrugged. "Do you want us to bathe or leave?" He pantomimed taking off his clothing then walking into the water.

The man shook his head.

He looked to Kimi. "What does he want us to do?"

A roar sounded in the jungle, far enough away to not scare him, but close enough to remind him danger was around the next tree. They needed to get home before dark—before the predators had all the advantages.

"I think he wants to know why we're here," she said. "These are his lands. My lands." She smiled. "These are my ancestors. Lakota Sioux Wolves."

The other two lumbered up beside the man with

the shawl, crossing their arms and scowling. One of the men had a shock of black hair twice as thick and spiky as any he'd ever seen. The Wolf man contorted his face into an ugly glower, his dark eyes giving an even darker warning.

"I don't know how you know they are *your* ancestors." He clasped her hand and squeezed. "They look nothing like your people."

"I can feel that they are. You know how sometimes you can sense things that aren't obvious on the outside? Well, that's what I mean."

He nodded. "Yeah, I understand."

The leader repeated his gesture, and the other two mimicked him, pointing to them then the river.

What could they want?

Nika held up Kimi's arm, showing the Alpha her bandage. "She's sick." He pointed to the wrap. "We're here in your time to get help. Save her from the Wolf virus." He knew they didn't understand his words, but what else could he do? They'd come so far. It wasn't fair to be thwarted right before they traveled back to their own time. If they hadn't been so exhausted, he'd tell Kimi they should make a run for safety.

The man scowled and came closer, motioning his men to follow. He reached for her arm.

She drew back, and Nika tensed.

"She's sick," he repeated. "Don't hurt her."

The man pointed to himself. "Trryr." Then pointed to Nika and Kimi.

Nika looked out over the strips of late afternoon sunshine. This beautiful, deadly world was going to be more deadly as soon as night fell. He should cooperate, so they could get out of there. He took a deep breath.

"Nika," he pointed. "Kimi."

"Bnnn." Trryr pointed to the Wolf man on one side. "Cttoh." He pointed to the Wolf man with the thick, black hair and scowl.

Nika dipped his head in a slight bow of acknowledgment.

"Kimi." The man pointed to her arm. "Sick."

"Yes!" Nika looked at him. Trryr picked up on language. Or maybe he knew more than he was letting on. "Sick." He put his hand on Kimi's elbow. "Pain." He winced, covering his own discomfort. As soon as they got back to the present and out of danger, he'd tell her.

Trryr nodded and held out his hand to her. She presented her shaking arm, and he tugged at the bandage.

He set the dirty knife on the ground then flicked at the edges of the bandage, softening the adhesive and peeling the cotton away, strip by strip. She flinched when the open air hit the sore. Trryr held her shoulder, and she composed herself, biting on her lower lip to avoid making a sound.

He smiled. His mate was strong.

When the binding had been removed, Nika grimaced at the violent purple-and-yellow color swirling around the angry-looking wound. Trryr sniffed the sore then wrinkled his nose and muttered something to his men. They headed over to the meadow.

Trryr pulled her toward the warm pool and looked back. Nika followed.

"What's he doing?" Kimi's eyes widened. "Is he going to toss me in the water?"

"I don't think so." Nika said. "Maybe he plans to wash off your arm."

"Yeah."

Trryr kneeled in the mud at the water's edge and

held her arm out over the steaming pool. He cupped his free hand and lifted the heated water to her arm, pouring handful after handful over her sore. She closed her eyes.

"Does your arm hurt?" Nika kneeled beside her and put his hand around her waist to steady her.

"No." She laid her head on his shoulder. "It feels good."

"How good?" He kissed the top of her ear. "Something you might want to repeat—"

Suddenly, she was yanked up, and Nika barely had time to get to his feet before Trryr had her sitting on the rock beside the pool. He climbed up beside her on the rock. If only they could get some time alone together. Without diseases and saber-tooths and giant mammoths and dire wolves and time travel. Would he ever get a chance to get to know her better somewhere safe?

She smiled at him, and the heat from her gaze went straight to his groin. Yes, they'd get through this, figure out the future, and be together as mates. These little obstacles weren't going to stop them.

Trryr's men returned with *saxifrage* blooms and piled them on the rock in a purple pouf of sweetness.

"Why would they bring these flowers?" she asked.

"They must know the flowers are the cure to the sickness." He watched Trryr. He had total authority, yet he had to speak little to his men to get his point across. A quiet, yet strong leader. Not unlike Drew.

"How would they know? And what are they going to do with them?"

"I don't know. But none of these Wolves seem infected with the virus, so maybe they've dealt with the sickness before."

Trryr chewed a handful of flowers, then another, shoving his mouth full as he could each time then spit them into his palm. He reached for her arm then smeared the paste onto her sore, coloring the skin an even deeper blue-purple. She looked away, her thin face hidden behind her hair. He hoped with every fiber of his being the flowers would heal her. Was the cure so simple? Trryr spit the rest of the flower onto the ground then bent to drink from the pool.

"You okay? How's it feel?" He examined the sore, prodding at the boundary of the medicine. "That mess looks awful."

"Tingly. But better, I guess. Not burning or

anything."

"Okay, let's hope the medicine works. We'll have to watch. We still need to take some home for the rest of the pack and your tribe and check with Wen because I'm pretty sure she wanted to make a tea from the blossoms." He didn't trust these men, but he knew he had to pretend to. So far, there wasn't a reason not to.

Trryr stood and wiped the water off his mouth.

"Thank you," she said. "The medicine feels wonderful."

Trryr smiled a violet smile and nodded. A large bird with a wingspan of at least twenty feet soared over the meadow, casting a long shadow. Trryr and his men crouched and watched the bird retreat.

"It does feel better, Nika." She held her arm up and studied the wound.

Trryr pointed at her sore then at Nika and scowled. "Sick." He pointed.

Crap!

He'd had no intention of letting Kimi know he was infected, so he shook his head.

Trryr scowled and sniffed around him. "Ni-ka sick."

Busted.

"What's going on?" Kimi asked. "Why's he smelling you? Why's he saying you're sick?"

"I don't know." *Crap, crap, crap.* "He's wrong. Must have me confused with someone else."

Trryr's face lit up. He grabbed Nika's knee and pointed at his thigh. The other Wolf men gathered around, and he waved them back. "Ni-ka. Pain."

She scowled. "Tell me what's going on."

"Yes, yes, okay." Nika unzipped his pants and pulled them to his knees.

"What!" Kimi's eyes went wide. "Why are you taking your clothing off?"

"He knows I'm infected. Senses the sickness somehow." He sat on the rock and pushed his jeans to his ankles. "I'll let him treat me now. Get it over with."

"You didn't tell me." Kimi turned away. "How long have you known?"

Trryr and his Wolf buddies snickered, and Nika shot them a stern look.

Trryr chewed a wad of flowers like he was chewing popcorn at a movie, absorbed in the events unfolding in front of him.

"I didn't want to worry you."

"You should've told me. I don't appreciate being lied to." Her voice hitched on a sob.

I'm an ass. Nika swallowed. "You had a lot on your mind, and you were in a lot of pain yourself. Wasn't like you could do anything to fix it, and I didn't want you blaming yourself for me getting sick." He reached for her but she pulled back.

"I suppose not." She tugged at her hair. "But I'd prefer to have been given the choice to make a decision how to react at least."

Cttoh said something to Trryr in their language, and Trryr laughed.

"I should have told you. I'm sorry." He adjusted his pants. "At least I'm wearing underwear."

She rolled her eyes. "Don't hide things from me again, Nika." The sheen of her tears catching the last rays of sunlight cast rainbows across his vision. "I don't give my trust easily, and I rarely offer a second chance."

"I'm sorry. I promise I won't."

Smack.

He jumped as Trryr whacked him with the wet flower compound. Maybe the Wolf man thought he liked it rough.

Trryr pointed to the wet mess then to Kimi and then walked off to the edge of the pools with his men. Nika winced when pain shot up his leg. Thank goodness Trryr had noticed he was infected, too. He and Kimi might not have reached Los Lobos in time.

"Guess he figures my mate can spread it for me." He attempted to smile at Kimi. "My *female*."

Kimi took a deep breath. "Don't push your luck. I may not be from your time, but I'm no simpleton."

"I know." Nika grinned. "Be gentle with me."

"I will. Unless you keep teasing me. Then I'll poke you."

"It hurts."

Her brown eyes widened. "I know."

"Yeah, you do, don't you?" He couldn't imagine, even with his own pain, how she must've felt—stuck out in the forest alone, trying to find a cure, suffering. And from another time to boot. It was a miracle she was alive.

She reached out with one finger and touched his leg near the edge of the flower paste, and he doubled over from sensation. She yanked her finger back. "I'm sorry! Does it hurt that much?"

He shook his head and willed his dick to calm down. Her soft touch on his leg had sent an electric jolt straight to his balls, and if she saw the result, he'd be humiliated. "Gimme a second," he muttered. "The medicine's cold, that's all."

Judging from her reaction, she didn't have a clue what had happened, thank goodness. He rubbed his face and thought of the tiger's stinky breath and rotting carcass.

Deep breaths.

"Don't be a baby." She watched him. "I need to spread the medicine. Look at my arm. I barely feel any pain. It's healed a lot."

He peeked at her arm. The sore had dried up, and her skin was only faintly blue—and maybe from the stain of the flower. "Wow. That's amazing."

He straightened his leg, so she could do her work. He should spread the salve himself, but he wanted her to touch him, no matter what his body's reaction was.

Her touch...so good.

Mate.

Claim her.

She slid her finger through the gooey mess again,

and he let out a groan and leaned his head back. She rubbed in circles, spreading the salve over his thigh.

Sticky, and cool.

He looked at her, into her brown eyes framed with thick, dark lashes. She smiled. "Feel good?"

Her mouth moved, but he wasn't sure she spoke aloud. She ran her tongue over her lips, and he placed his hand behind her neck and pulled her into a kiss. Muddy hair and all, she'd never been so beautiful, so *his*. Her tongue sought his, and he pushed back, wanting to be in charge. She smiled against his lips and straddled him, probably getting the flower paste on her legs, too.

He didn't care.

The pressure of her legs against him and her ass against his barely clad and very erect cock pushed him into a haze of dizziness. He slid his hands up her back, wishing he could pull her sundress up and off. Exhaustion, pleasure, pain, all became one feeling. A howl curled at the back of his throat, and he tipped his head back....

"Ni-ka."

He startled. Trryr stood over them, arms crossed over his chest. Cttoh scowled beside him. Kimi moved off him and onto the rock, a flush of embarrassment tinting her warm brown skin. He stood, then pulled up his pants over his bulge and zipped, avoiding eye contact with Trryr and Cttoh. He felt better than he had all day, though every muscle ached with overuse, and he didn't want to deal with any scrutiny or teasing. He was with his mate and acting like any adult male would.

He held his hand out and helped her up.

"Thank you," she said.

He smiled. "Any time." He leaned in to whisper in her ear, "Any time."

"Ni-ka," Trryr said.

Nika sighed and turned. Trryr pointed to where the hills met the sky. A fat, orange sun sank below the apex of the hill, shooting out a few faint orange rays across the land. Nika looked back to Trryr, who now pointed in the opposite direction, back toward the Wind Cave. He pointed to Kimi and Nika and made a hurried "follow me" gesture.

He shook his head no. They had to get back to Gee. Where were his pack and the bag of flowers? He spotted them on the edge of the clearing. He'd get them then they would rush back to the opening in the cave where they arrived and get the hell out of here. A light breeze pushed by, sending the stem over the water pools out over the meadow.

Trryr frowned. He pantomimed eating and drinking, and Nika looked to Kimi.

"I know we need to go back to take care of our people, but it's the least we can do, don't you think?" she asked. "And when else will we ever get a chance to dine with the dire wolves? We'll be safe, and we can leave after we eat. Won't delay us much at all."

He turned to Trryr and nodded and pointed toward the Wind Cave. Trryr smiled and spoke to his men then started walking toward the meadow in the direction of the cave. Nika took Kimi's hand and grabbed the sack of flowers and his backpack.

"Wait," she said. "My shoes."

"And my knife." He moved to get the blade and stuff it into his pack.

Trryr stopped, but the other Wolf men ran into the meadow, falling into wolf shape before they reached the tree line. She grabbed her shoes from the rock and slipped them on, taking one last look out over the river. He smiled and held his hand out to her.

"Let's go have dinner with our ancestors," she said.

Trryr walked ahead, turning to look back and see if they followed. The first splash of stars traced across the darkening eastern sky, and Nika grabbed Kimi's hand. The day had turned out so much better than expected, and after a good meal, they would head home. Drew and Gee would be proud of him for saving both Kimi and the pack.

Ryker might even tell him he did a good job.

Chapter Eight

Maybe her expectations had been too high, but dinner wasn't what she'd anticipated. Not even close. Kimi watched the men chewing the last of the stringy meat from the saber-toothed bones. The room in the cave was large yet not overwhelming, and dark and dingy would have been a nice way of describing the space. Bones littered one side of the cave, and when the Wolf men finished eating a piece of meat, they tossed the bones onto the pile.

She'd have enjoyed the meal more if she'd been able to shift, but Nika had agreed they should wait a little longer to make sure their sores would stay gone before they risked Wolf form.

Nika leaned against her. He hadn't eaten much of the food either. He'd tasted and picked enough to not appear rude to their hosts, and she'd sensed he'd been as uncomfortable as she was. Trryr and his Wolf men sat on the dusty cave floor, chattering and talking in their confusing language, some dozing off, and some cleaning their few tools—axes, spears, and clubbing instruments. A huge fire had once burned on the blackened hearth—somehow vented above—but now the flames flickered and the conversation slowed. The men began turning over to sleep right where they had eaten, covered by straw mats or strips of fur.

"We should go soon," she said. "Gee will be waiting on us. Though I think it would be nice to stay here a while...you know, if we didn't have responsibilities."

"Yeah." Nika yawned. "And this fire is so warm. It's making me sleepy, and I hate the idea of getting out in the cold night air. Gimme a few minutes, okay? We'll head back soon."

She nodded. She studied the cave ceiling, marred by the tarred and blackened remains of many fires. Movement caught her eye, and she watched a few smaller wolves pass by in a cave corridor running behind the vaulted room. Who were they? Were they shifting wolves, or another species? With all the emotions she got in this room of shifted dires, she couldn't sense the little ones running by at all.

She put her hand on his shoulder and shook him. "I'll be right back."

"Are you going outside?" He reclined on the floor on his backpack. "If you can wait, I want to rest a few minutes and then I'll go with you."

"No, I'm not going outside. I want to look around this area of the caves." She stood. Most of the men were dozing. "I'll be back in soon. I'm not going far."

"Okay, I'll be here." He closed his eyes. "Be careful."

"I will." She watched her mate sleep. How could anyone fall asleep so fast after the stresses they'd had? She smiled. Wouldn't be long till she was sleeping next to him every night—once she explained things to her father.

She'd worry about all of that tomorrow. Right now, she needed to find out who the little wolves were and what they were doing. They were much closer in size to her own Wolf. Maybe they were her direct ancestors. Whoever they were, they were beautiful.

If only they never had to leave. She could live the simple life—even find food she liked, if she had the time. This world was paradise—so different from the harsh reality that awaited them back in their own days.

She crept around the sleeping men, trying to avoid waking them, though if their own snoring didn't rouse them, a mammoth's stampede wouldn't. The cave floor had bumps and ridges where generations of men and Wolves had slept, and she wondered how many had called this exact spot in the cave system home. With the pungent odors of perspiration, rare cooked meat, and ash, she wouldn't have trouble finding her way back.

Once she was in the low-hanging passageway where she saw the wolves race by, she stopped and waited for her eyes to adjust to the half-light. Good thing her human sight was excellent because the cave was illuminated with faint streaks of color. She wasn't even sure how. Scratching sounds and muffled noises came from around the next corner, and she crept along the latticed rock wall toward the sounds. Then clearer voices, low and lilting, bubbled up. The voices spoke the same language she'd heard Trryr and his men speaking but with softer clatters and tones.

She-Wolves!

Shifted to human, bare-breasted women with long, brown-and-black hair and the lovely tan skin of Native Americans sat talking in a circle, all naked except for a wrap about the waist and decorative beaded jewelry.

Kimi smiled. “Hello.”

The women scattered. In a flash of fur, they tumbled into Wolves and sprinted away, leaving nothing except silty paw prints and thin clouds of dust in their wake. Had she scared them away, or did they not want to talk to her? Why? She shook her head. At least now she knew the pack had women. Well, of course they did—they stayed on the fringe.

Quiet and out of sight.

But why had they run? She wasn’t going to hurt them. In fact, she had more in common with them than their menfolk. She wanted to talk. Maybe they didn’t realize she was also a shifter. Maybe they didn’t know she could shift into a Wolf. Kimi sighed. Whatever the reason, they were gone now, and she needed to get back to her Mate. Being alone in the caves was a little unnerving.

She turned to go and ran face first into a hard, smelly chest with long, stiff hair.

She didn't have time to scream before strong hands grabbed her upper arms and pain shot through her where fingertips bruised on contact. She tried to pull away, but the Wolf man held her tight. Adrenaline shot through her, and she kicked at her attacker. He held her out at arm's length where she couldn't do any damage.

"You're hurting me!" she said, struggling. "Let me go!"

He shoved her against the moist cave wall then pushed against her, pinning her on the rock's surface.

Kimi screamed.

Cttoh put his hand over her mouth and smiled, his foul breath coming in sickening waves in her face.

She closed her eyes and brought her knee up into his groin. With a yelp, he released her arms, doubling over and falling to the cave floor. She kicked him in the face as hard as she could then turned to run.

He grabbed her by the ankle and yanked. She fell to the cave floor face-first, her hands breaking her fall. Still bent over in pain, he pulled her toward him, lifting her dress up as he did.

She screamed and kicked her legs, and he ran his hands up her dress and squeezed her thigh.

Out of nowhere, Nika was on Cttoh, pummeling him with his fists.

"Be careful!" she called.

Cttoh let her leg go, and, free, she backed away. Trryr and a few men dashed into the little open area and grabbed Cttoh while Nika gave him one more punch.

"Did he hurt you?" Nika growled, panting. "I'll—"

"No, but he was going to—"

"Cttoh!" Trryr yelled and pointed.

Kimi jumped and held onto Nika while Trryr shouted instructions. His face was a shade of reddish purple she hadn't seen in his world, and she could tell he was beyond angry.

His men dragged Cttoh out of the room. Trryr tapped her on the shoulder, and she peeked at him.

"Sssorry." He tilted his head then motioned her to follow.

She tried to smile, but her energy was gone. "In a minute, Trryr. Give me a minute to recover."

He held her, wrapping her in his arms. "I almost

killed him."

"I almost let you."

"What if I hadn't heard you?" He shook. "What if...?"

"You saved me. Thank you."

"No need to thank me." He pulled her tight. "We're leaving soon, I promise. Once I figure out how to get out of this cave, we'll find the area we need to go to."

"Do you remember what the vent looks like?"

He looked into her eyes. "Of course I do. Let's find out what Trryr wants to show us then I'll figure out how to ask him where the cave exit is."

"Let's go, Trryr," Nika said. "What do you want to show us?"

Trryr headed out into the corridor and into a smaller offshoot. They followed, trying to keep up with his fast steps.

A gurgling scream echoed through the cave, and she clutched Nika. He held onto her. "What was that?"

Trryr didn't even turn around. "Cttoh."

She covered her mouth, and Nika nodded. They continued down the passageway in silence. Whatever the men had done to Cttoh, it hadn't been good. In the near-dark, Trryr ambled along like someone who knew every inch of the cave system, which he probably did, and she tried to follow in his footsteps. The toll of the day's stress and physical exertion had weighed her down to the point of complete exhaustion. If she had to run to escape something again, she would lie down and offer herself as sacrifice. At least her arm seemed to be healed.

"How's your leg?" she asked.

"I don't feel any pain," he replied. "I hope the infection is gone for good, not just latent. And I hope we have the same luck with the people that need the cure back home in our own times. It's too easy."

"I hardly call the battles we've faced easy. And I wish we didn't have more to fight in our own times. I wish I could be with you without all the struggle...."

He tugged the backpack up onto his shoulder. "Me, too."

Trryr slowed, and they stopped to avoid bumping into his back. Ahead, the cave narrowed a bit, the lacey formations on the walls wet and shiny.

Where was the light coming from?

To the right lay the opening to another

passageway, the entrance bathed in golden light. Trryr motioned them ahead. She took a deep breath and followed.

Maybe this was the way out of the cave.

He held onto her shoulder, and they followed Trryr to the opening of the lighted passageway. Whatever the men had done to Cttoh hadn't been enough. Nika had failed again—he should never have fallen asleep and let his mate go wandering through the cave by herself in a new and dangerous place. Nothing to do with her being a girl—he had no doubt she could take care of most things on her own, as the smack on the head had proven—but it was irresponsible of him to sleep when danger lurked everywhere.

So much for impressing Drew and Gee. And if Ryker ever found out...well, he'd never earn the Enforcer's trust or respect.

He hung his head. He had so much to learn. Failure would be his teacher once again. Was he always destined to be a student?

"Look!" Kimi's shoulder tensed.

When he gazed into the passageway, he saw a room carved out of the cave. One section held an oval-shaped steaming pool with a low, curved hammock of rock overhanging. The hot springs must continue under the caves, though only one pool bubbled up in this room.

It made sense. The area around the cave was formed by hot springs, and the spring itself originated in the Wind Cave.

"Wow," was all he could muster. The room rivaled a five-star spa.

Along the far wall was an elevated limestone hearth with a small, warm fire burning and lapping at the air, a neat stack of wood beside it. Far above and at an angle, the smoke tracked out of a hole in the side of the cave, forming a semi-walled chimney. Good thing they weren't trying to hide from anyone—the mountain probably looked like lit Swiss cheese from outside.

On the floor in front of the fire lay a pile of plush furs. Nika looked at Trryr, and the Wolf man raised his eyebrows. Nika shifted his gaze away.

"I think they want us to stay here tonight, Nika!" She clasped her hands together. "What do you think? One night can't hurt, right?"

"I...." He squirmed. The last thing he wanted was

an audience for their first night together.

Thousands of rose quartz crystals lined the back edge of the warm pool, and the fire cast them in a pink glow, like tiny celestial flowers.

"We can go home in the morning." She sighed. "We'll be rested, and the cure should be in full force by then—if the speed the medicine's worked so far is any indication. Besides, I've never seen anything so beautiful. And I'm tired. What's the harm in getting some rest before we go back?"

He looked back to Trryr who was now grinning like the wolf who swallowed the canary. The Wolf man had no shame. He tried not to grin back. Who knew the dire wolves had a sense of humor? "Well, I could use a bath."

"You and me both!" She coughed. "I mean...."

"Yes, you and me both." He took her hand and rubbed the back of it with his thumb. "We'll stay. Let's see if we can get some privacy." He slid off his backpack and set it on the ground. "Thank you, Trryr. You can go now." He shooed him away with his hand.

Trryr dipped his head again to Kimi—something Nika doubted he rarely did to a female. He pointed to a woven basket filled with what appeared to be leaves and flower petals, and then a smaller one piled high with fruits, with a carved bowl filled with water beside it. Then he ducked out of the room, closing off the doorway with a pale skin forming a makeshift curtain tucked around the protrusions in the cave formations.

He looked at Kimi.

They were finally alone.

Chapter Nine

"What are you doing?" Nika gulped.

Kimi had slipped out of her shoes and dropped the muddy dress onto the ground. "I thought we were taking a bath. She turned toward him, her arms covering her breasts. Her lips curved into a smile, and she peeked at him through a fan of dark lashes. "Aren't we?"

"But...."

"What?" She turned to the pool, slipped her fingertips into her underwear, and slid them off, revealing a firm, round ass, golden brown in the flickering firelight. "Don't you want to bathe...with me?"

He growled and moved toward her, but before he could grab her, she was in the water, sending up a splash of warm wetness toward him.

He shed his T-shirt, well aware she was examining him. Holding in his stomach, he slipped off his shoes, socks, and muddy jeans as fast as he could.

Deep breath. Face her while I take off my boxers or turn away?

What would Ryker do?

He saw what must be amusement flash in her eyes. Wasn't she the one who was supposed to be from a different era, where women were demure about mates and claimings? *Awkward. Why am I the awkward one?*

A splash of warm water hit him across the torso, and her clear laugh rang out when she struck the surface of the water again. Droplets landed across his boxers.

"Hurry up!" She bobbed out of the water, her dark hair floating like snake grass atop the surface of the pool.

Anxiety forgotten, he tugged his boxers off and tried to walk toward the pool with as much swagger as he could muster with his dick pointing at the cave ceiling. He had this.

He tripped.

He almost sensed the fall right before it happened, but he definitely felt it as it did. His feet slipped right out from under him on the wet floor, and he tumbled headfirst into the pool. He pondered staying underwater to hide his embarrassment, but he popped up, and the first thing he saw was her face.

Her eyes wide, mouth open, he didn't give her the chance to laugh—but pulled her into a kiss, her wet body going limp in his arms. He searched for her tongue with his. His erection pressed against her soft stomach, and his Wolf paced, moaning to be set free. In a flash, he could flip her over, slide in, and then bite her shoulder....

No!

She pulled away from his kiss, wrapped her legs around his waist, and tugged him forward. "What's wrong?"

"Nothing's wrong." He ground his teeth. "I want you. So much. Since I first saw you, my body's been telling me to make you mine. I can't wait much longer, butterfly, but I want everything to be right. I need to know this is what you want, and that we aren't mating because we have to because of instinct."

She slid close, her sex rubbing against his. "I want you. Not because we're instinctually mated. It's more than that. We're two halves from differing time periods, yet we fit together perfectly. Meant to be. I feel it."

"And the kisses are great." He grinned, hoping he hid his nervousness.

"Yes." She splashed him in the face. "The kisses are great."

He pushed her wet hair away from her face. "We should slow down. We don't have to rush."

"So let's not. We have tonight. Then we have to get home to help our people." She shoved away, sending a wave of warm water across his chest. "Let's see what's in the basket."

They dumped out the large leaves and soft petals onto the ground beside the steamy pool. The firelight played along the lacy cave walls illuminating swirls of orange and red petrified lava. With the soft steam and crackling fire, the scene looked like a fairy temple, magical and sacred. He held her hips and leaned against her back, letting his dick ride up the line of her ass. The warm water slid along his skin as he moved, sending shivers of pleasure along his legs and back. Near-nirvana.

"Wonder what the petals are for?" She held up a translucent red star-shaped petal. "These aren't the ones that cured us."

"I know what they're for." He grabbed the petals by the handful and sprinkled them over the top of the bubbly water, sending the sweet and fruity scent of the ancient flower across the cave.

"Oh, that smells so nice." She closed her eyes and inhaled, tilting her head back and inhaling the heady aromas.

He watched her wet breasts rise and fall with her deep breathing, then picked up a large leaf from the basket, its green surface beaded and rough, and dipped it into the warm water. He dragged the edge across her shoulders. "Feel good? I think they use these for cleaning cloths."

She nodded and pulled up her hair out of the way. "Seems to work. Please clean the rest of the mud off my back. It's itchy."

"Gladly."

He scrubbed the large leaf halfway down her spine to where the heated water met skin then she rose up and he went farther down, feeling the bumps and ridges of her flesh. She moaned when he rubbed the back of her thighs and knees under the water.

"Yes, they must wash with those," she whispered. "My back tingles cold even in the warm water."

"I think it's a mint plant of some kind." He ran the leaf down her healed arm. "My hand feels icy cold."

He dropped the leaf into the water, letting it float away with the flower petals then grabbed her hips and tugged her close, running his hand down the front of her legs and feeling her body tense then relax in his grip. He explored the folds of her sex with his fingers. She spread her legs to give him more access and he pulled her closer. He took his time, feeling along the slit, yet not entering, rubbing and flicking at her bundle of nerves until she collapsed into his arms.

"More," she panted. "Please." She pushed against his hand. She closed her legs over his fingers, and his Wolf threatened to burst through to get at his mate.

Howling wasn't an option. This wasn't going to end until he took her.

"Slow down," he said. "I want to see all of you when I claim you."

"Then let's get out of this pool." She climbed out, water running down her torso like crystal rivers across a dark landscape.

"Sit down." He surprised himself with the calm power of his voice. No more anxiety. He knew what to do and how to do it. Relax and let things happen. His Wolf knew.

She sat and dangled her legs in the warm water, and he pulled her ankles toward him until her ass was even with the edge of the pool. The flickers of firelight across her naked body sent him into a frenzy inside, but he remained calm and collected. He'd tend to his mate first.

"Lie back," he said.

"It's chilly." She covered her breasts with her arms and chill bumps spread across her stomach.

"Not for long."

She lay back on the smooth edge of the pool, her legs falling open a bit as her back arched to the ground, and her nipples hardened. She shivered.

"You're such a beautiful butterfly." He moved a hand up each thigh, and she raised her head and shoulders off the ground. "Lie back."

Her body trembled under his touch, like a thin

paper in the wind. Soon, they'd be warm by the fire, but right now, he needed to see her—all of her. He pushed her legs apart and ran his thumbs up each side of her sex, parting the lips and uncovering the wet pink center. Her knees shook, but she didn't stop him, so he leaned in and blew, letting his warm, wet breath settle over her exposed sex.

As if by their own accord, her legs flew out to the side, giving him full access. He plunged his tongue low then licked her from bottom to top, stopping to focus on her clit, flicking it over and over again with firm strokes.

A strangled cry escaped her lips long before he expected, signaling she was falling over the edge of bliss. He sucked hard, trying to catch the essence of her pleasure in his mouth and fly with her in her bliss. She closed her knees around his head and he kissed and nipped at the inside of her thighs.

When her breathing had slowed, he climbed out of the pool, scooped her into his arms, and carried her to the furs in front of the fire. Her body still trembled with aftershocks and she held onto him tightly.

"Are we bonded?" she whispered.

"Not yet, butterfly." He set her down and stood by the fire to dry off. He'd have to claim her before long, or his body would never forgive him. But if he hurt her by rushing things, he'd never forgive himself. "Soon."

"How soon? I feel like there's a need inside that isn't quenched—even though that was amazing. Please, I want to mate."

He put two more logs on the warm fire, listening to the same crackling and popping fires made ten thousand years later. "I don't want to hurt you," he said. "Sometimes the claiming—"

"I want it." She sat up. "Please, Nika, come lay with me."

If his dick had to be asked again, it was going to hop off and go on its own. He sighed and moved to join her on the furs. The soft furs, dense and thick, soothed his skin and aching muscles but did nothing to ease his passion.

"Lie back." She pushed his shoulders. "My turn."

"But—"

"Only fair."

He lay on his back. When her hand wrapped around his dick and squeezed, he tensed. "Not too hard," he said.

"Show me." She looked into his eyes.

He cupped her hand in his and stroked, long and slow. "Feels good."

And it did. But not so good he'd make a mess and ruin the claiming. She pushed his hand away.

"What if I do this?" She jerked harder and faster, and he felt a buzz beginning at the base of his balls.

"Too hard," he said. "Slower." He couldn't ruin a perfect night.

She moved her hand away. "Okay, well, close your eyes, and I'll do the slow thing."

"You prefer to be in charge, don't you?"

She smiled, and he shook his head then closed his eyes. He waited on her hand, anticipating the softness of her grip. When her hot mouth closed over the head of his dick, he about lost it. He sat up and pulled her to him.

"I can't wait any longer," he said. "Are you sure this is what you want?"

"I've never been more sure about anything."

He kissed her then pulled her to her knees and crouched behind her. "I'll be gentle."

"Don't."

He knew the first time could be painful for females and he didn't want to hurt his mate, but she was testing his reserve. He was pretty confident she was a virgin, even if she acted like she knew everything. Of course he'd had sex, but he'd never claimed a female, so he was in new territory, too. He took a deep breath. "Ready?"

"Yes!"

The exasperation in her voice was the last straw. He positioned himself behind her and held her hips and pushed. She grunted and pushed back several times, but he wasn't making progress. He pushed again, cold fear running through him that he might be hurting her. Sweat broke out along her spine, and then she raised her backside and slammed into him.

Fuck.

If anything had ever come close to feeling as good as being inside her, he couldn't name it. More than running on swift paws through the forest, or shifting at his mind's command, or even howling with every fragment of his soul, this was right and good. He fell into her until sparks of pleasure rose from his groin and her muffled cries became loud shrieks of *yes, yes, yes*, and then his dick quivered and poured his passion into her as he bit down on her shoulder, marking her, his and he, hers.

Mine. The tang of blood filled his mouth.

Mates.

Forever bound.

He howled.

Chapter Ten

Kimi put on her second shoe and smoothed her mud-caked dress over her knees. Too bad they hadn't thought to clean their clothing in the pool so the fabric could dry overnight, but mating had taken priority over clean clothing.

As it should.

"Ready to go home?" Nika asked. "I know it's early, and Trryr was pretty insistent. I don't feel I rested a full night...."

"I'm ready." She laughed. "We have so much to do before we can relax again. Though last night—"

"Was great!"

"Yes." She stood, turning to take one last look around the cave where they had spent their evening. She'd miss the cuteness of the place, but she was looking forward to a regular bed—even a pallet in her own time, as long as he shared the bed with her.

She frowned. Getting her father to accept him wasn't going to be easy. Cross culture—cross time, even—would be a huge challenge. When the Alpha saw the two of them, he'd know Nika had claimed her. She pulled her thick hair back. Maybe he'd be happy enough Nika had saved her that he wouldn't kill him on the spot.

"What are you thinking about, butterfly?" He tipped her chin up and looked her in the eye.

His deep-green gaze seemed to be made of the purest green stone, and she leaned in to steal a kiss from his lips. "Nothing much. I'm wondering how we're going to get the cure back to my people and if we'll be in time to save them."

He put his cheek against hers, and she savored the warmth and closeness and the brush of his curls against her neck. "It'll be fine, you'll see. Gee will help us, like he helped us here."

"I hope you're right."

"Aren't I always?"

She scowled. "One night and you think you are always right?"

"Yeah." He grinned and batted his eyes.

"No, most definitely you aren't right."

"Well, I still think Gee will help us."

"He will, but it has nothing to do with you being right. We'd better get going."

She pulled back, and Trryr was standing in the cave's makeshift doorway, holding the fur curtain. He motioned them forward.

He grabbed his pack with the flowers and then headed out with Trryr. She tagged along behind them, dragging her fingertips along the cool cave walls. They didn't pass a single Wolf man on the way, and it didn't seem to her they went down the same tunnels they took the night before. Where was Trryr taking them?

Maybe she'd been too tired to notice, and this was the same route.

No, this was *not* the way—the ceiling was too low. She bent over to avoid hitting her head on the cave ceiling, and the drips of iron-red watery sediment came more often. They crept along in silence, moving when necessary and aware of each step. The path rose in a steep grade and began cutting back on itself inside the mountain as it went higher and the cave narrowed to a single-file space. Pebbles tumbled down the passageway behind her, shaken loose from their footsteps on ground that couldn't have been walked on in years.

Complete darkness swallowed them by the time they reached what must have been the top of the path, and they felt along the narrow passageway by hand. Everyone's heavy breathing sounded ten times as loud and echoed in the constricted area. Trryr grunted, and motioned them to go ahead of him. Soon, the side of the mountain opened up into a small boulder-sized hole, and fresh air whooshed in.

She crawled out through the opening onto the mountainside and stared up at the sky of the past, filled with a hundred million stars staring back. On the cusp of dawn, the sky was at its most gravid with possibility. Nika stepped out behind her, then Trryr.

"My God, so beautiful," Nika said.

"I can't believe how many stars you can see."

The cricket song all but deafened her, loud and piercing, but somehow, the sound fit in with this over-the-top world.

Trryr grunted and stared with them at a large meteorite that flamed overhead, bisecting the sky in a trail of orange fire.

"Thank you, Trryr," Nika said. "For everything."

Trryr nodded and pulled out a leather scroll and pushed it into Kimi's hands.

He turned to go, and Nika caught him by the arm. "Hold on." He pulled the knife out of his bag and held it out. "Take this. The least I can do for all your help."

Kimi nodded at Trryr, who'd looked at her for approval. He smiled the largest smile they'd seen from him, took the knife, and then crawled back into the caves.

"He turned out to be very helpful." She linked her arm in Nika's. The view from the mountain showed the orange mist of dawn beginning to spread across the eastern horizon, and, in the far west, the stars faded.

"Very." He tied the flower sack onto his backpack and pulled the pack onto his shoulders. "We wouldn't have survived this without him."

"How do we get out of here? We're nowhere near where we were when we came."

"Time to start hiking." He headed toward the path down the mountain.

“Wait, I want to see what’s on this scroll.” She unrolled the first turn of the leather.

“We can look at it when we get home.” He kept walking. “Let’s go.”

“Nika....” She called. What could the words mean? She unrolled the scroll the rest of the way. “Nika!”

***

Nika leapt, his jowls flapping as he landed with a thump on the path in front of him, the backpack and scroll tight in his teeth. Soon, he’d be all the way down the mountain and near the Wind Cave entrance. The cool, fresh air of morning blasted his lungs more than any energy drink could ever do, and the bright streaks of sunlight through the pines on the mountain were like direct shots of electricity as he bounded through them.

He was going back to Los Lobos. *Home.*

He stopped at the large, crooked pine on the north face of the mountain, a sheer cliff dropping off at his paws, and waited. Where was she? She’d been right behind him when they ran down the mountain, and he'd heard her howl when she shifted.

There she is! Mate!

Her deep black fur glinted in the dawn's light like a thousand black diamonds, moving, alive with femaleness and mystery. She howled, her muscles undulating along her back, her tail high.

He trotted to her, and they nuzzled, the backpack and scroll dropping to the ground while they celebrated. She smelled of smoke and fire and pine. His. She pawed at him, leaping in circles—daring him to try to catch her. He'd mount her now if they weren't waiting....

A gigantic shadow spilled over the ground, and he and his mate stopped. The bear moved with purpose, then bent to pick up the leather scroll Nika had read earlier, scrawled with the line drawing of a bear, a raven, a mountain, two howling wolves, and a distinctive letter "G."

Nika wagged his tail. Gee would understand the markings. He would get them all back to Los Lobos safely. Trryr had somehow known about Gee. Life was mysterious—and magical.

A raven cawed, circling a spot near the base of the mountain. Gee grabbed the scroll and the backpack and nodded for them to follow. Wen was showing them the way home.

Even in victory, the pack needed each other's help to survive, and it had always been that way—even in the time of the dire wolves.

Kimi leapt beside him and licked his cheek.

Nika howled.

Epilogue

Nika watched Wen preserve the last of the purple flowers in her water canner. Once they were cool, he'd take them to be stored in the basement at Gee's Bar. The Bear was right—canning was a great way to preserve them, and a perfect way to carry some for the trip to Kimi's time to save her people. No one in Los Lobos had gotten sick in the ordeal, though Drew had made everyone drink Wen's *saxifrage* tea just in case. He didn't know if Ryker would ever forgive him for the bitter-tasting cure. But everyone had admitted if he hadn't found her in the woods, the whole town could have been infected, and it might have been too late to find the cure.

Nika was a hero.

Now, he had to prove it to Kimi's father.

About the Author

Kerry loves history and spends large amounts of time wondering about people who lived and walked on Earth in the past.

In addition to writing, she's a college instructor, costumer, painter, and editor. Her new love is her Mini Cooper Convertible, Sheldon, and they have already gone on many adventures. Her family currently has seven cats (two Bengals and five rescues), a panther chameleon, a lionhead miniature bunny, and a leopard gecko.

For the latest news (and lots of contests) be sure to sign up for Kerry's newsletter at http://eepurl.com/1T6PX.

Follow her on Twitter (@kerryadrienne) and Instagram (KerryAdrienne) for lots of cat pics!

Made in the USA
Monee, IL
29 May 2022

97206881R00085